the land of promise

A PLACE TO CALL HOME
BOOK THREE

THE LAND OF PROMISE

AL & JOANNA LACY

Multnomah Publishers

THE LAND OF PROMISE
© 2007 by ALJO PRODUCTIONS, INC.
published by Multnomah Publishers
a division of Random House, Inc.
International Standard Book Number: 1-59052-564-7

Cover photo by Jeff Vanuga/Vanuga Photography

Printed in the United States of America
Multnomah is a trademark of Multnomah Publishers and is registered in the
U.S. Patent and Trademark Office.
The colophon is a trademark of Multnomah Publishers

For information:
Multnomah Publishers, 12265 Oracle Boulevard, Suite 200,
Colorado Springs, CO 80921

Library of Congress Cataloging-in-Publication Data
Lacy, Al.
  The land of promise / Al and JoAnna Lacy.
    p. cm. — (A place to call home ; bk. 3)
  ISBN 1-59052-564-7
    1. Cherokee Indians—Fiction. I. Lacy, JoAnna. II. Title.
PS3562.A256L36 2007
813'.54—dc22

2006031469

07 08 09 10 11 12 13 14 — 10 9 8 7 6 5 4 3 2 1 0

We dedicate this book to our dear friend, Gayle Sawyer,
former legal administrator at Multnomah Publishers.
Thank you, Gayle, for being such a blessing to us.
We love you.
Al and JoAnna
2 Timothy 4:22

preface

n the sixteenth century, the Cherokee Indians occupied mountain areas of North Carolina, Georgia, Alabama, and Tennessee. They had a settled, advanced agrarian culture. In 1540, they were visited by the Hernando De Soto expedition, and the Spanish explorer later reported that he was impressed with the Cherokee people.

In 1820, the Cherokees adopted a republican form of government, and in 1827 they established themselves as the Cherokee Nation.

By 1832, much pressure was being put on the government in Washington DC, to move the Indians elsewhere so that white people could have their land. This, coupled with Andrew Jackson (who was known to be prejudiced against Indians) being president of the United States at the time, spelled doom for the Cherokees as the pressure mounted for the removal of all Indians to the West. There were five tribes known as the Civilized Tribes: the Cherokee, the Chickasaw, the Choctaw, the Creek, and the Seminole. These five tribes were slated to occupy the land in the West known as Indian Territory.

The Cherokee Nation's leading chief, John Ross, a mixed-blood Cherokee, struggled hard against President Jackson's administration to keep his people from being put off their land.

Ross's struggle continued when Martin Van Buren became president in 1837. The opposition was too great, however, and as the story was told in the first book of this trilogy, *Cherokee Rose*, in the winter of 1838–39, some fifteen thousand North Carolina Cherokees were forced by the U.S. Army to make the one-thousand-mile journey westward to Indian Territory, which is now the state of Oklahoma. This harrowing journey, during which more than four thousand Cherokees died, has become known as the Trail of Tears.

The Cherokees of Georgia, Alabama, and Tennessee had already been forced to go to Indian Territory, also having lost their homes. The same thing was happening to the people of the other four Civilized Tribes.

Repeatedly forced to surrender their lands, the people of the Cherokee Nation, as well as those of the other four tribes, were hoping to find in Indian Territory "a place to call home."

prologue

wo outstanding Cherokee chiefs lived during the period of history covered in the first two books of this trilogy, *Cherokee Rose* and *Bright Are the Stars*. Their names are still revered today by the Cherokee Indians: Chief John Ross and Chief Sequoyah. Because they also appear in this book, we include here some background information about these two men who made history in the Cherokee nation.

John Ross was born October 3, 1790, near Lookout Mountain in the Smoky Mountains of North Carolina. Born of a Scottish father and a mother who was part Cherokee, the blue-eyed, fair-skinned John Ross (whose Cherokee name was Tsan-Usdi) grew up as an Indian. Courageous and highly intelligent, Ross became the leader of the Cherokee resistance to the white man's planned acquisition of land the Cherokees had lived on for centuries. Because of Ross's valor in fighting for his people, he was made a Cherokee chief at the young age of twenty-two. Since he was mostly white, though in his heart he was all Cherokee, the chiefs of every Cherokee village in the Smoky Mountains voted to honor him with a second name: Chief White Bird. He married a full-blooded Cherokee woman named Quatie and in 1819 was voted in as president of the National Council of Cherokees.

With the threat of the Indians' forced move to the West hanging over their heads, John Ross put up a spirited defense for his people. His petitions to President Andrew Jackson, under whom he had fought in the Creek War (1813–14), went unheeded. On May 28, 1830, the U.S. Congress, following Jackson's leadership, established the Indian Removal Act.

In 1838–39, when Martin Van Buren was president, Ross had no choice but to lead his people, under duress from soldiers of the U.S. Army, toward an unknown western prairie called Indian Territory. On the journey, his wife, Quatie, took sick and died.

Sequoyah was born c. 1773 in North Carolina, and was called Sogwali by his parents. After both parents died while he was yet a youth, some Bible-preaching missionaries to the Cherokee people named him Sequoyah.

Having been a Cherokee chief for five years, in 1809 Sequoyah began working to develop a system of writing for his people, believing that increased knowledge would help the Cherokee Nation maintain their independence from the whites. By 1821 he had developed a system of eighty-six symbols that made up the Cherokee alphabet. The simplicity of his system enabled students to learn it rapidly, and soon Cherokees throughout their nation were teaching it in their schools and publishing books and newspapers in their own language, printing them on their own presses.

Chief Sequoyah had a great interest in the Bible, which was introduced to him in English by the same missionaries who renamed him, and by 1823 he had translated the entire Bible into the Cherokee language, and thousands of copies were printed.

In 1825, the General Council of the Cherokee Nation presented Sequoyah a silver medal for these accomplishments.

introduction

n 1838, General Winfield Scott of the United States Army arrived in Cherokee territory of the Smoky Mountains of North Carolina with seven thousand soldiers to prepare the people for a journey that would become known as the Trail of Tears. (This story is told in the first volume of this trilogy, *Cherokee Rose*.)

During the long, difficult trek westward, the Cherokees found that many of the soldiers were brutal toward them. However, one young soldier, Lieutenant Britt Claiborne, did his best to protect the Indians from the brutality. His kindness soon drew the attention of Cherokee Rose, a young Cherokee maiden. As the journey progressed, Britt and Cherokee Rose fell in love. Knowing they would have to part once they arrived in Indian Territory, they began to pray for a miracle from God that would allow them to stay together and become husband and wife.

During the journey, over forty-two hundred Cherokees died, and in March 1839, the surviving ten thousand Cherokees arrived at Fort Gibson in Indian Territory. General Scott officially turned the North Carolina Cherokees over to Fort Gibson's commandant, General Austin Danford, and the soldiers who were there to keep all the inhabitants of Indian Territory under control. Scott then had a private talk with Britt Claiborne and told him that since he was a quarter Cherokee, he was eligible to serve on the Cherokee Police Force in the Territory.

Britt applied for a police position, and because of his background as an army officer, he was hired. When Britt told Cherokee Rose, they praised the Lord for this answer to prayer. God had given them their miracle.

In the second volume of this trilogy, *Bright Are the Stars*, Britt and Cherokee Rose were wed, and Britt proved himself valuable as a police officer, saving the lives of innocent people and bringing criminals to justice. Britt and Cherokee Rose were also blessed with children, Bradley Allen and Summer Dawn. Britt eventually became Indian Territory chief of police, and the family moved to Tahlequah, the Cherokee national capital.

The Cherokee people found genuine happiness in Indian Territory and came to love their new home. The revered and tenderhearted Chief Sequoyah often said that because his people were happy in their new home, to him the stars at night shined with a new brightness.

In July 1885, Craig Parker and his wife, Gloria, lived on their farm some five miles south of Joplin, Missouri. One day, Craig was stunned when the sheriff and two deputies showed up on his doorstep and arrested him for robbing the Joplin National Bank. Though Craig was innocent, he went to trial and was sentenced to fifteen years in prison.

Early in January 1889, Britt Claiborne received a letter from Benjamin Harrison, president of the United States, informing him that Congress had devised a plan to set boundaries for the habitation of the Indians in what had been their territory for over fifty years. The land within the boundaries would be called "reservations." The president said he would be sending troops to the District to make sure the Indians were resettled on the land assigned to them.

The United States government would then allow white people to enter Oklahoma District and claim some 2 million acres of "unassigned lands." The white settlers would be allowed to claim 160 acres of land per family. Those who lived on and improved their claim for five years would then receive title to it.

In the last week of that month, every newspaper in the United States carried the announcement about the Unassigned Lands Bill. The announcement emphasized in bold print that on April 22, the army would oversee a "land rush."

In February 1889, young widow Martha Ackerman, her three children, and her parents, Will and Essie Baker, left Wichita, Kansas, in the Baker wagon, heading for Oklahoma

District, excited about the prospect of having a new home with 160 acres to farm.

At the same time, just outside of Amarillo, Texas, Lee and Kathy Belden and their two sons drove away from their farm, which was being repossessed by the Panhandle National Bank. For two years, the drought in the Texas panhandle had taken its toll on the Belden farm, as well as on many others in the area. Lee and Kathy were optimistic about going to Oklahoma District to get a fresh start.

In late February 1889, the man who actually committed the bank robbery for which Craig Parker had been convicted confessed just before he died. When Gloria Parker arrived at the Missouri State Prison to be reunited with her soon-to-be-released husband, Craig told her of reading about the upcoming land rush. He wanted to go to Oklahoma District and start over. Gloria happily agreed with his plan. They would leave Missouri in time to look over the land before laying claim to their new farm.

one

n the third week of February 1889, young farmer Lee Belden and his wife, Kathy, were headed southeastward across north Texas in the family's covered wagon. On the driver's seat with them were their sons, nine-year-old Brent and six-year-old Brian.

There were a few scattered clouds in the azure sky, being tossed about by the same cold wind that was blustering across the dusty plains. The Beldens were dressed warmly, and a heavy blanket was spread across their laps and legs. They had been following the rail-road tracks ever since leaving Amarillo three days previously. Lee hoped to make it to the town of Childress before sundown.

The two horses bent their heads against the wind, puffing as they pulled the wagon along the bumpy dirt road.

The wind howled and whined. It flapped Lee's hat brim and snatched at his upturned collar with icy fingers. The boys kept their faces deep into their wool collars, and Kathy caught her breath when a particularly strong gust whipped at the swaying wagon. She tightened the strings on her wool bonnet and sighed deeply as a shiver passed through her.

"What's the big sigh for, sweetheart?" Lee asked, turning to look at her.

"Oh, nothing."

Lee grinned and chuckled. "Come on, now, I know you better than that. You don't sigh like that unless something is bothering you."

Kathy's gloved hand came out from under the blanket that covered their legs, and she patted his hand that held the reins. Her smile was quick and warm. "You think you know me pretty well, don't you?"

"Well enough to be positive that a big sigh like that has to mean something."

Kathy was silent for a few moments as the wagon rocked on, then another sigh escaped her lips.

Lee fixed his eyes on her. *She's still the prettiest woman I've ever seen. Pretty as a delicately carved cameo.* He reached down and captured her gloved hand in his. "Come on. What is it?"

"Oh, honey, it's nothing, really," Kathy said. "It...well, it's just that I expected this land east of us to be better than the

Amarillo area where we came from. But it looks as barren and
desolate as our farm did."

Lee squeezed her hand. "Well, my love, we aren't in
Oklahoma District yet. After all, we're only three days from
Amarillo. The land hasn't had much of a chance to change yet.
You just wait and see. From what I've read and been told about
Oklahoma District, you'll love the rolling hills, the thick stands
of trees, the rivers, the streams, and in the springtime, green
grass and wildflowers in abundance. It's still February, so nothing's in bloom yet. Give us a few weeks and some warmer
weather, and I'm sure you'll be pleasantly surprised."

She smiled and said, "I'm sorry, honey. Guess I'm in too
much of a hurry to get to our new home and get settled in. I'll
be more patient. I promise."

"Good girl." Lee leaned over and placed a kiss on her rosy
cheek.

Suddenly, Brent pointed ahead and said, "Papa, look up
there! That freight train that passed us about an hour ago is
stopped on the tracks!"

As the Belden family drew nearer, they could see three
crewmen laboring to remove a dead horse from the tracks right
in front of the train. More dead horses were lying at the same
spot on the tracks.

Lee's eyes bulged. "What in the world is this?" He quickly
put the team to a trot, and the three crewmen looked up at the
covered wagon as it drew to a halt. Lee hopped to the ground
and helped Kathy down as the boys also clambered down.

As the Beldens approached the puffing crewmen, who
were sweating in spite of the cold wind, they saw that they had

a rope tied around a dead horse's neck, struggling to drag it off the tracks. They saw, then, that four more horses were lying dead on the tracks and that one other dead horse had already been dragged away from the front of the engine.

The crewmen paused in their effort as Lee said, "Looks like the train hit these horses."

"It sure did," said the oldest of the three men. "I'm Ray Hebert, the engineer. A dozen or more wild horses came up out of that gully over there, just ahead of the engine. I hit the brakes while my fireman, here, blew the whistle. But the engine struck these six, killing five of them instantly. The one that was still alive was in bad shape. I had to use my rifle to put him down."

"I see," said Lee, taking a step closer. "Could you use some help?"

Hebert grinned. "Well, yes, Mr.—"

"Lee Belden. This is my wife, Kathy, and these are our sons, Brent and Brian."

"Glad to meet all of you," said the engineer. "My fireman, here, is Darren Connor, and that's Nathan Tunget, our watch-man."

The other two crewmen and the Beldens exchanged greet-ings, then Ray Hebert asked, "You folks from around here?"

Lee shook his head. "No, sir. We're from the Amarillo area. Farmers. But we're on our way to Oklahoma District. We're going to claim one of those pieces of farmland the government is going to turn over to white folks when the land rush takes place on April 22."

"Pardon my inquisitiveness, but why did you leave the Amarillo area?" Hebert asked.

"Well, you must know about the drought in that area this

past year. It was so bad, especially where our farm is located, that we had some serious crop failure. We ran into some financial trouble, and the bank foreclosed on us. We just got too far behind on our payments."

The engineer shook his head. "That's too bad, Mr. Belden. I'm really sorry about that."

Lee removed his hat and ran his fingers through his thick black hair. "Tell you what, fellows. How about I unhitch my team from the wagon and we use them to drag the rest of these dead horses off the tracks?"

Ray Hebert's face brightened. "Good idea, Mr. Belden! Let's do it!"

With the help of the Beldens' horses, the tracks were quickly cleared. As Lee was hitching the team back onto the wagon, Darren Connor said, "So, Mr. Belden, which part of Oklahoma District are you hoping to settle in?"

Lee pulled at an ear. "Well, Mr. Connor, we're going to go all the way to the east side and enter near Tahlequah."

Hebert frowned. "Why are you traveling so far when there are entrances on the western border?"

Lee pulled at the same ear again, and Kathy and the boys smiled at each other, knowing what was coming.

"Well, Mr. Hebert, I want to get as far from the Texas drought as possible."

"I can understand that, after what you've been through." Hebert scratched the back of his neck. "Mr. Belden, with the distance you and your family are going to have to travel to get to the Tahlequah entrance, you'll never make it by March 2. Most of the land will have been inspected by the other settlers by the time you get there."

"Yeah," Lee said wearily, "but I don't see that we have any other choice."

"Tell you what, Mr. Belden. We have an empty flatbed car and cattle car. We could get your wagon up the ramp onto the flatbed car with our pulleys, and we can put your horses in the cattle car. This train goes all the way across north Texas through Wichita Falls to Texarkana. We could let you off about twenty-five miles west of Texarkana, and that would give you a straight shot northward up the east border of Oklahoma District to the entrance just east of Tahlequah. You'd get there in plenty of time to look the land over."

Lee saw the excitement in the eyes of his wife and sons. He stuck out his hand, and Hebert met it. "Thank you, Mr. Hebert. This will really help us!"

The engineer gripped Lee's hand tightly. "Hey, glad to do it! You certainly helped us get those dead horses off the tracks, so we'll be able to get the train moving a lot sooner than we would have."

"You and your family can ride in the caboose with me," Nathan Tunget said. "With this cold wind we've got, you'll be warmer in the caboose than in your wagon, believe me."

"We appreciate that, Mr. Tunget," Kathy said.

"We sure didn't expect to be takin' a long train ride on this trip!" Brian said.

"Yeah, me an' Brian ain't never been in a caboose before!" Brent said.

"It is wonderful," Kathy said. "We'll take food out of the wagon so I can cook on the woodstove in the caboose. You *do* have a stove in the caboose, don't you, Mr. Tunget?"

"Sure do," Tunget said. "I'll build a fire in it right away so it'll be nice and warm in there."

After some of their supplies had been transferred from the wagon to the caboose, the Beldens looked on as the experienced railroaders loaded the horses into the cattle car, then used their pulleys to draw the wagon onto the flatbed car.

Within a few minutes, the train was moving speedily along the tracks with black smoke rising into the sky from the engine's smokestack. Nathan Tunget had built the promised fire in the caboose's woodstove while the Beldens settled in, and the warmth of it was welcome to Kathy as she stared out the window at the barren landscape. In her mind's eye, she dreamed of rolling hills dotted with patches of forest and covered with green grass and colorful wildflowers.

Also in the third week of February, Will and Essie Baker, their widowed daughter, Martha Ackerman, and Martha's three young children, Angie, Eddie, and Elizabeth, were in the Bakers' covered wagon about to pass by Winfield, Kansas, on their way south to the Oklahoma District border. A cold wind was blowing underneath a partly cloudy sky.

The three children were inside the wagon, sitting on the floor at the canvas opening just behind the driver's seat. Essie was seated next to her husband as he held the reins, and Martha was on her mother's right, running her gaze over the flat land.

Martha was excited about what lay ahead for her parents, her children, and herself, but there was also a sadness deep in her heart. It was a disturbing thing to be leaving Wichita, where she had been born and raised and where her beloved husband had recently been buried. She missed Troy so very much.

Tears began to film Martha's eyes, and she bit her lower lip to keep from crying. *Life will be better for us in a fresh, new place*, she assured herself.

She picked up the newspaper that lay on the wagon seat beside her. Holding the recent issue of the *Wichita Chronicle* firmly so the wind could not snatch it out of her hands, she let her eyes focus on the small article in the lower right-hand corner of the first page, which quickly caught her attention. Her eyes covered the article in a hurry.

"Oh, no!" her parents heard her say.

"What's the matter?" asked her mother, glancing at the paper.

"Well, we're going to have to drive farther than we thought to enter Oklahoma District. It says here that the official entrance just south of Silverdale City is not going to be in service. The closest one is near the little Kansas town of Tyro."

"Hmm, that's another sixty miles east," Will said. "I wonder why they aren't using the one that was supposed to be south of Silverdale City."

"It doesn't say, Papa. Just that it won't be there as previously announced."

Will sighed. "Okay, then we'll head that direction right now rather than waiting to turn east when we get to the border. We'll at least cut off a few miles that way."

As he spoke, Will guided the horses off the road, angling the wagon southeasterly across the rolling fields toward Tyro.

The western horizon was coming alive with a golden color,

sending a reddish-gold hue through a small patch of trees just ahead. The earth, the sky, and the low clouds that hung over the west were bathed in brilliant, breathtaking light.

Suddenly, four-year-old Elizabeth left her siblings inside the wagon and climbed onto the seat next to her mother. "Mama! Mama! Look what God painted for us! Isn't it bootiful?"

"Yes, little one, God certainly painted a *bootiful* picture for us this evening." Martha kissed the child's cheek and held her close, enjoying the warmth and the sweet scent of her.

Moments later, Will pointed ahead. "There's a creek right up there, Essie. Some other travelers are taking advantage of it."

All eyes in the Baker wagon were drawn to the spot where three wagons were parked on the creek bank. The men were watering their horses, and the women were getting ready to cook supper at a fire that was sending out puffs of smoke.

Will drove the wagon up to the bank of the gurgling creek and stopped a few yards from where the other travelers were gathered. The women at the fire smiled and waved to them, as did two of the three men who were watering the horses.

"Look like friendly folks," Will said. "Let's go meet them."

They all alighted from the wagon and walked toward the other travelers. Warm greetings were exchanged, and they learned that two of the wagons were owned by couples who appeared to be in their sixties: Alfred and Barbara Decker and Donald and Jennifer Wooley. The third wagon was owned by Gilbert and Corrie Gerson, who appeared to be in their midthirties and had their teenage daughter, Peggy, with them. Gilbert was an obese man, and though he was not unfriendly, he never smiled. Martha and her parents told the three families that they were from Wichita and were on their way to the entrance to the Oklahoma District just south of Tyro to establish a new home.

Alfred Decker, who had an exceptionally bright smile, said, "Looks like we've all got the same thing in mind. The Wooleys, the Gersons, and Barbara and I are all farmers from the Chanute, Kansas, area, and we're headed to Oklahoma District for the same reason that you folks are."

Donald Wooley looked around at his traveling partners and said, "I think we ought to invite these folks to travel with us the rest of the way to the Tyro entrance."

The others agreed, and the Bakers and Martha happily consented.

Later that evening, Martha sat in silence, staring blankly into the flickering flames of the campfire, her mind in the past as she thought of the dreams and plans she and Troy had made for their life together.

Soon, a sleepy Elizabeth snuggled up beside her mother and yawned. Martha took her into her arms, and within a few minutes, Elizabeth's head began to droop, and she was fast asleep. Martha placed a kiss on her little daughter's head, stood up with her in her arms, and said to her parents, "I think I'd better put this child to bed."

The two other children were on their feet, and Martha looked down at them. "Come along now, Angie and Eddie. It's bedtime for you, too."

Angie and Eddie kissed their grandparents good night, and soon Martha had all three of them on their pallets inside the wagon. Elizabeth was sound asleep, but the other two each prayed as their mother held their hands.

Martha returned to the fire and sat down facing her parents. She retrieved her tin cup of tepid coffee and took a sip.

"I guess they're all three in dreamland," Will said.

Martha smiled and nodded. "No need for a bedtime story tonight. They're really tuckered out."

Martha took another sip and stared into the dying flames.

After a long, quiet moment, Essie bent her head to catch Martha's eye and asked, "Are you all right, dear? You've been exceptionally quiet ever since we left home."

Martha managed a smile. "Yes, Mama, I'm all right. I've just been a little melancholy since we left Wichita. I've been thinking about all the plans Troy and I had made for our lives."

"Oh, I'm sorry, dear," said Essie. "I—"

"Don't apologize for asking about me, Mama. It's all right. I'll get adjusted to Troy being gone pretty soon. I really am looking forward to settling somewhere new and different. I'm sure it will be good for us all. It's just that—well, sometimes it's hard to leave the past behind."

"We both know that, honey," Will said. "But everything's going to get better for us."

"Of course, Papa. It will."

Essie scooted toward her daughter, took her hand in her own, and said, "The Lord is with us, Martha. He'll take care of us and help us as we establish our new home on one of those big sections."

"I know He will, Mama."

Will rose to his feet. "Well, my dears, I think it's time we follow the children's example and get some sleep."

two

verything was on schedule the next morning when the four families had breakfast and the dishes were done. The sun had already tipped the eastern horizon rosy red, and the open land toward the south lay fresh and colorful in the morning light as the travelers were about to climb into their wagons.

Alfred Decker took hold of his wife's hand to help her onto the driver's seat when something moving on the prairie caught the corner of his eye. He froze in place, then suddenly shouted, "Indians! Southwest!"

Every adult eye in the camp flicked that direction to see a band of Indians coming over a rise about a half mile away, riding their horses hard straight toward them. They began whooping as they raised their rifles over their heads.

"Osage!" Will Baker cried out. "They're fierce! If you men have guns, you'd better get them!"

"We don't have a chance, Baker!" Gilbert Gerson said. "There are at least a dozen of 'em!"

"We can't just stand here, Gerson!" Will said as he took his rifle from the wagon seat. "We've got to fight 'em! Women and children, get under the wagons! Quick!"

Alfred Decker and Donald Wooley both spoke their agreement with Will Baker and grabbed their guns.

Gilbert Gerson grabbed his own rifle and told Corrie and Peggy to get under their wagon, muttering loud enough for everyone to hear, "We don't have a chance! Not a chance!"

As the four men cocked their rifles and took cover, the terrified women tried to comfort each other and the equally terrified children beneath the wagons.

Martha and Essie scooted up tightly, surrounding the children, and as the thundering sound of the Indians' galloping horses grew louder, Martha said, "We're going to pray right now and ask the Lord to protect us!" Martha closed her eyes and said, "Lord, we need Your help right now! Please! Please! You can do anything! In Jesus' precious name I beg You! Stop those wild Indians now!"

The four men took aim at the approaching Indians, waiting for them to draw within range. Suddenly a rifle roared above the sound of the whooping, followed by a few other shots. Then a great number of guns roared behind the Indians.

Also distinguishable was the sound of a Gatling gun spitting out its deadly lead in rapid fire.

The four men beside the wagons looked on wide-eyed at the army unit of at least two dozen men on horseback behind the Osages, plus the wagon that carried the Gatling gun, which was coming at them from another angle.

The Osage leader shouted an order to his warriors, and they quickly turned and headed east, leaving five dead warriors behind. The riderless horses galloped away with the fleeing Indians.

The soldiers sent more bullets after the Indians until they disappeared over a hill, then their commanding officer turned his horse and led his men toward the wagons.

As the women and children were coming out from under the wagons, little Elizabeth Ackerman shouted, "Mama! It's gonna be okay! God heard your prayer!"

"Yes, sweetheart," Martha said with a lilt in her voice. "He did hear my prayer. The Indians are running away, and the soldiers are here to help us. Praise the Lord!"

"Oh, praise God!" Will Baker shouted. "He sure *did* answer your prayer, Martha!"

With the fear gone from her eyes, Angie took hold of her mother's hand as everyone watched the soldiers draw near. "Mama, those Indians are really bad, aren't they?"

Martha patted her head. "They are, honey, but you must remember that there are bad white men, too. The Indians used to live freely on this land, but white men came and took it over, making the Indians live on reservations. We can't really blame them for feeling hostile toward us. We need to pray for them."

Angie nodded. "I'll pray that they don't come back, whooping and hollering again."

Elizabeth pressed close to her mother, and Martha pulled her other two children close to her and sent a silent prayer of thanksgiving heavenward.

When the cavalrymen drew up with the army wagon behind them, their leader ran his gaze over the faces of the small group of travelers and said, "I'm Captain James Lambdin. Is everybody all right?"

"Looks like we are, Captain," Will Baker said. "We sure are glad you and your men showed up when you did. You're a real answer to prayer."

The captain adjusted himself on his saddle. "I don't know if we're an answer to prayer or not, but I'm glad we got here in time to drive those Indians away."

"Where are you from, Captain?" Alfred Decker asked.

"My men and I are from Fort Hays, further west here in Kansas. We're headed for Baxter Springs to meet up with troops from other forts. The Osage have been attacking white people as they travel over this part of Kansas, and the army is preparing to take control and bring the killing of white people to a halt."

"Well, we sure are glad you showed up when you did," Donald Wooley said.

The captain smiled. "Where are you folks headed?"

"We're headed for Oklahoma District," Will Baker said. "Gonna join the land rush to claim our 160 acres of farmland."

"And where are you planning to enter the District?"

"At the official government entrance just south of Tyro."

Captain Lambdin glanced at the lieutenant who was sitting his horse next to him. "I think we'd better persuade them to go to the Tahlequah entrance so we can escort them."

The lieutenant nodded. "I agree, sir. There could be plenty more Osage warriors between here and Tyro."

"What is this other entrance you're wanting to persuade us about, Captain?" Will asked.

"It's called the Tahlequah entrance, sir. It's an official government entrance that'll be opened on March 2 for prospective settlers such as you and your friends here. It's a few days' ride south of the border where Oklahoma District and the state of Missouri meet. You'd travel south on the Oklahoma District–Missouri border for some thirty miles, then along the border of Oklahoma District and the Arkansas state border the rest of the way. The Tahlequah entrance is about fifty miles farther south, due east of the town of Tahlequah, which is close to Fort Gibson."

Will smiled. "I know about Fort Gibson, but I've never heard of Tahlequah."

"Well, it's been there for several years. Since my men and I are going to Baxter Springs, we'll escort you to where the Oklahoma District border meets the Missouri border, and then you'll turn south. You'll be safe from any more Indian attacks then. There are no wild Indians in that area at all."

Will nodded, then turned to look at the other travelers. "Sounds good to me. How about the rest of you?"

All the adults were nodding.

"Good!" Will turned back to the captain. "All right, sir. We'll happily accept your offer to escort us."

The travelers expressed their appreciation to the captain and his men, and as the four families headed for their wagons,

Will Baker praised God for sending the soldiers to save them from the Osages and to escort them safely.

Gilbert Gerson scowled at Will. "Baker, God didn't have anything to do with sendin' these soldiers to our rescue."

Will stopped in his tracks, batted his eyes in surprise, and asked, "Why do you say that?"

"Because there *is* no God! We just got lucky, that's all!"

The others looked on wide-eyed as Will said, "There is no God, eh? Well, are you not aware that there's a natural, irrefutable law in this world that every effect has a cause?"

Gilbert licked his lips. "What do you mean?"

"Look around you, and look at yourself. This universe, this world, and everything in this world is an effect. *God* is the cause if this effect."

Gilbert wheeled and walked away, saying over his shoulder, "I don't wanna talk about it!"

Soon the wagons were rolling with the military escort surrounding them.

Corrie Gerson was sitting next to her husband on the seat of their wagon, with Peggy at her side. She turned, looked her husband in the eye, and said, "Gil, I wish you'd keep your atheism to yourself. You embarrass me when you talk to people like you just did to Will Baker."

"It embarrasses me, too, Papa," said Peggy, looking past her mother at the solemn face of her father.

Gilbert flashed them both hard looks. "Since nobody can prove to me that there is a God, my belief is the sensible one."

Mother and daughter exchanged glances, then Corrie said, "I suspect if Darwin could come back from the dead, he'd tell you your belief isn't so sensible."

"Well, since he can't do that, it doesn't make any difference what you think. I don't want either of you talkin' to people about it, as I've told you before."

Mother and daughter went silent.

Cook-fires were lit just after the travelers and their army escorts stopped for the night some three miles west of Baxter Springs, Kansas. Pleasant aromas filled the air.

At the Baker–Ackerman fire, little Elizabeth stayed close beside her mother while Martha and Essie were cooking the meal. Martha noted that Elizabeth kept looking out into the gathering darkness that surrounded the camp. Her sky blue eyes seemed to show apprehension.

After supper, Will, Essie, and Martha sat around their fire, talking about their future in Oklahoma District. Angie, Eddie, and Elizabeth sat in silence, listening. Elizabeth was cuddled up close to her mother. Martha again noted the foreboding look in Elizabeth's eyes as she kept looking beyond the fires into the gloom. She silently prayed for wisdom, asking God to help her comfort the little four-year-old, and to dispel her fear.

After a while, Martha looked around at her children and said, "Well, my dears, it's bedtime."

"Mama, can I sleep with you tonight?" Elizabeth said.

"Well, certainly, honey. But something's bothering you. What is it?"

The child threw herself into her mother's arms. Her voice quavered as she said, "Oh, Mama, I'm afraid those Indians are gonna come back in the dark! What if they do?"

Martha held her tight and said, "Sweetie, listen to me. The

soldiers are here, and they would protect us if the Indians came back. But more important, our heavenly Father is here with us, and He will keep watch over us. Nothing can get past Him."

"God is much stronger than those Indians, isn't He?" she said as the terror in her eyes faded.

"Yes, sweetie. He is indeed."

A smile parted Elizabeth's lips. "Then we're safe, aren't we?"

"We sure are, sweetheart," Will said. "The Lord is watching over us."

"I feel better now," Elizabeth said. "But could I still sleep with you tonight, Mama?"

Martha smiled. "Of course you can."

Will and Essie said good night to their daughter and grandchildren, then watched as they climbed up into the covered wagon. Will and Essie were sitting across from each other, with the campfire between them. Will saw tears in her eyes. He rose from where he was resting, stepped around the fire, and sat down beside her.

Tears were now glistening on Essie's cheeks.

Will put his arm around her, pulled her tight against him, and said, "What is it, darlin'? Why the tears?"

Using the back of her work-roughened hand to wipe away the tears, she gave him a small, weary sigh. "I…I guess my nerves are still a little on edge, honey. It's not every day that we face wild Indians. I was just thanking the Lord for sending the soldiers and for sparing all of us…especially the little ones. I have never been so frightened in all my life."

"Well, I can certainly understand that," Will said. "I was plenty scared, too. You know, though, I can almost sympathize with those poor Indians. They've been so mistreated by white men in this country, especially in the past several years. They've been lied to, and our government has broken one treaty after another with them. Most of them have never heard of the true God and of His Son. They only have their heathen religion. Of course it's wrong of them to try to kill us, but it really isn't hard to see why they act toward us white folks the way they do."

Essie nodded. "You're really something, you know that? We were almost killed today, yet you can understand and sympathize with the Indian people. It's no wonder I love you so much. Thanks for encouraging me to be more understanding toward them."

Will smiled. "I hope someday soon there can be real peace in this country between us and the Indians."

"Me, too. I'd rather not have to face any more angry Indians for the rest of my life! I can do without that kind of excitement."

"Amen to that, sweetheart. Amen to that!"

The next morning, Captain James Lambdin and his men escorted the travelers all the way to the northeast corner of the Oklahoma District border, where it met Missouri's western border. While sitting his horse, the captain wished them all a good life in their new homeland.

Just then the travelers and soldiers saw a young couple in a covered wagon coming from the north. The man pulled the wagon to a halt close by the captain and asked, "Is there a problem here, Captain?"

Captain Lambdin explained the situation to him.

"I'm glad to hear you were able to keep these people from

harm, Captain. My name is Craig Parker, and this is my wife, Gloria. We had a farm near Joplin, Missouri, but like these people, we're on our way to claim one of those 160-acre sections of land when land rush day comes."

A smile broke over Will Baker's face. He looked around at the others in the traveling group and asked, "Would you all agree to invite Mr. and Mrs. Parker to travel the rest of the way with us?"

Everyone quickly spoke their agreement.

"Thank you, folks," Craig Parker said. "We really appreciate this."

Will spoke for the group one more time, thanking the soldiers for saving their lives. Good-byes were said, and the travelers watched as the cavalrymen rode away, followed by the wagon bearing the Gatling gun. Within a few minutes, they rode around a bend and passed from view.

Among the group, a look of longing followed the soldiers, and Will sensed the fear that seemed to grip them. With a prayer in is heart, he said, "Now, folks, the captain told us we have nothing more to fear. We're in safe territory as we travel the borders of Missouri and Arkansas to our final destination. God has been so good, and we need to trust Him as He continues to keep His hand on us."

Craig Parker touched his elbow against Gloria's arm as she sat on the wagon seat and said, "I like those words, sir! The Lord will indeed keep His hand on us!"

Will looked around at the group and saw a smile on every face but that of Gilbert Gerson. Will nodded and said, "Well, let's get going!"

As the wagons rolled out, traveling southward along the

Oklahoma District–Missouri border, Will Baker sensed a genuine feeling of tranquillity among the travelers. They agreed just to eat snacks for lunch so they could keep moving, and at midafternoon they stopped at a creek to water the horses, then continued on.

That evening they stopped to camp for the night, and after supper was prepared, they sat down to eat together. The Deckers, the Wooleys, and the Gersons looked on as the Bakers, the Ackermans, and the Parkers bowed their heads and prayed silently over the food. Once again, Corrie and Peggy Gerson exchanged glances when they saw Gilbert scowling at the praying people.

The next morning, the travelers were up at dawn. They had their breakfast; then while the women washed dishes, the men fed and watered the horses.

The sun was rising as the wagons were put in motion, and they headed south once again. Everyone felt the excitement of the new life ahead of them in Oklahoma District.

three

arly on Saturday afternoon, February 23, at the United Cherokee Nation police headquarters in Tahlequah, Oklahoma District, Officer Najuno was on duty at the front desk, working on some police papers as directed by Chief of Police Britt Claiborne.

Najuno's attention was drawn to the sound of clopping horses' hooves and the rattle of a wagon. He looked out the large window to the street and saw an army wagon from nearby Fort Gibson pull up, with two soldiers on the driver's seat. Beside the wagon, on horseback, was Lieutenant Wiley Riggins, whom Najuno knew quite well.

Najuno hurried to the door and pulled it open. He saw Lieutenant Riggins leave his saddle and walk toward him, a solemn look on his face.

"Good afternoon, Lieutenant," Najuno said.

"Hello, Najuno," Riggins said. "I need to see Chief Claiborne right away. It's very important."

"I am sorry, Lieutenant, but Chief Claiborne is not here. He has not yet returned from lunch." He paused, looking into Riggins's eyes. "What is wrong?"

"Come outside with me to the wagon."

Najuno was on the lieutenant's heels, and when Riggins led him up to the side of the wagon, Najuno saw two dead Cherokee men lying in the wagon's bed.

"You know these men?" Riggins asked.

"No, sir. I have seen them, I am sure, but I do not know their names."

"Well, their names are not important right now. These two men resisted the soldiers who came to remove their cabins from the land that is being prepared for the white settlers. They drew knives to attack the soldiers, and the soldiers shot them. I happened to be riding by and saw it happen."

Najuno bit down on his lower lip and slowly shook his head. "I hate to see this kind of thing happen."

One of the soldiers who had come in the wagon said, "Lieutenant, here comes Chief Claiborne now."

Both Riggins and Najuno looked up to see the tall silver-haired police chief drawing up. When the chief saw the two bloody bodies in the bed of the wagon, he frowned and looked at Riggins. "What happened, Lieutenant?"

Riggins described the incident to Britt Claiborne, explaining that he had seen it with his own eyes.

"I'll take the bodies to their Cherokee chief for burial," Britt said. "It will be up to Chief Pilando to keep his people from resisting the United States government's orders that all the Indians must be living on the reservation before March 2."

"Would you like for me to go along with you, Chief, so I can verify to Chief Pilando that I saw these two men attempt to stab the soldiers who were there to take their cabins to the reservation?"

Britt nodded. "I would appreciate that very much, Lieutenant."

Late that same afternoon, at the Claiborne cabin in Tahlequah, Cherokee Rose was busy preparing supper when she heard the front door open and the voice of her husband call out that he was home. She smiled to herself, slid the skillet of fried potatoes off the flame of the cookstove, and rushed to meet her still handsome, distinguished-looking husband.

In the entryway, Britt's senses were already alerted to the fragrant aromas from the kitchen, and he sniffed the air appreciatively. *Mmmm*, he thought, *unless my nose is failing me, we're having pinto beans with ham, fried potatoes, and cornbread. Life doesn't get much better than this!*

Britt was hanging his broad-brimmed hat and his black leather jacket on a clothes tree by the front closet when he saw his wife coming from the kitchen, a wide smile on her lips.

"Hello, sweetheart," said Britt, folding Cherokee Rose into

his arms. He kissed her soundly, then held her at arm's length. "You're just as beautiful as you were the day I married you!"

Cherokee Rose tweaked his nose playfully and said, "Even though we will have our fiftieth wedding anniversary on April 28 and I have wrinkles on my face to prove it?"

Britt kissed her again. "I don't see any wrinkles on your face. Those are *beauty lines.*"

She took him by the hand, and they headed toward the kitchen. They had taken only a few steps when they saw Walugo come from his room, which they had added to the cabin a year earlier. Britt and Cherokee Rose stopped and waited for the old man to meet up with them.

Walugo had lived in his own cabin in Tahlequah for several years, but when he was approaching his nineties, Britt and Cherokee Rose invited him to come and live with them. They had the room added onto the cabin so Walugo could have his privacy, but also because they wanted to take care of him in his old age.

"Something sure smells good!" Walugo said as he drew up to them, smacking his lips. "I am so glad I no longer have to eat my own miserable cooking." He gave his only daughter a pat on her back. "Yes, it is indeed a blessing to this old man to be living here with the two of you."

Cherokee Rose stroked his wrinkled cheek. "Father, we are the ones who are blessed. We so enjoy having you here. You took such good care of me when I was growing up. Now it's my turn, and I love it!"

"And so do I," Britt said. "Now, let's get to the kitchen and partake of that good-smelling food. My stomach is growling!"

"Mine, too!" Walugo said.

When they entered the kitchen, Britt told his wife and father-in-law about the two dead Cherokee men who had been killed when they resisted the soldiers who had come to remove their cabins to the new village led by Chief Pilando.

Walugo shook his head. "I hope our people will stop resisting the United States government. It will only produce more graves."

"You're right," Britt said. "As you know, I've warned them about this many times."

"Before the two of you wash up for supper," Cherokee Rose said, "I have some good news to share with you." She picked up a large brown envelope off the kitchen cupboard. "There is a letter in here from Bradley and Wilma."

"It must be quite the letter to have been sent in that large envelope," Britt said.

Cherokee Rose smiled. "They sent the large envelope because it contains the front page of the February 19 edition of the *Dallas Daily News*. Take out the newspaper, and tell Father what it says about Bradley."

Britt removed the front page of the newspaper from the envelope and read it silently. When he finished, he glanced at his wife, then looked at his father-in-law. "Walugo, you've heard of that infamous gunfighter Colby Slocum."

Walugo nodded. "Yes. A bloody, heartless killer. What about him?"

"This article tells how Slocum rode into Dallas on Monday, February 18, to challenge Dallas County Sheriff Bradley Claiborne to a shoot-out."

Walugo's jaw slacked and his eyes widened. "Well, since my daughter just said the letter came from *both* my grandson and his wife, it must have turned out all right."

"It did, thank the Lord. The article says that a week earlier, Sheriff Claiborne had been forced to shoot it out with Slocum's younger brother, Harry, and killed him. Colby went after Bradley to get his revenge. The article says that a crowd on the street in Dallas was watching when Sheriff Claiborne tried to talk Slocum out of forcing him to draw against him, but Slocum went for his gun, and the sheriff outdrew him. Slocum was buried before the sun went down that very day."

Walugo let out a sigh. "Thank God for protecting my grandson!"

Britt looked at his wife. "You said you had some good news to share with us. You weren't kidding."

"My grandson is to be commended," Walugo said. "And the Lord is to be praised."

"Amen and amen," Cherokee Rose said.

Britt then took the letter out of the envelope and read it aloud. In the letter, Bradley and Wilma expressed their appreciation to Bradley's parents and his grandfather for praying daily for Bradley as he carried out his job as sheriff of Dallas County. They declared in the letter that the Lord was answering their prayers.

Britt placed the letter back in the envelope, laid it on the cupboard, then put his arms around his wife and father-in-law, and said, "Let's pray."

They bowed their heads, and Britt thanked the Lord for sparing Bradley's life.

The next day, Sunday, February 24, just after twelve noon, Pastor Joshudo and his wife, Alanda, were at the front door of the church building in Tahlequah as the people were leaving after the morning service. In the line of people who were shaking hands with the pastor and his wife were Britt Claiborne, Cherokee Rose, and Walugo.

Prior to the service that morning, Britt and Cherokee Rose had shared the news with Pastor Joshudo about their son, Bradley, having been forced to draw against the infamous gunslinger Colby Slocum. At announcement time, the pastor had told the congregation about it and asked them to pray daily for Bradley Claiborne, asking God to protect him. Many of the older church members remembered Bradley as a boy.

Britt, Cherokee Rose, and Walugo drew up to the pastor in the line, and all three of them told him how much they liked his sermon and that they were pleased to see three people walk the aisle and receive the Lord Jesus Christ as their Saviour.

Britt patted his pastor on the shoulder and said, "Pastor, you are doing a wonderful job in your ministry."

Pastor Joshudo smiled modestly. "Thank you, Chief Claiborne, for your kind words."

Cherokee Rose put an arm around Alanda, squeezed her tight, then looked at the pastor. "Pastor Joshudo, with this wonderful wife at your side, it is no wonder that your ministry is such a success!"

The five of them had a good laugh, then the Claibornes and Walugo headed for the family wagon. As they drove the short distance from the church to their cabin, Britt said, "After dinner, I think I'll take a drive to the new Cherokee village just south of Tahlequah, which is under Chief Degalado's leadership, and see how things are going there. Would you two like to go with me?"

When they both said they would, Britt nodded. "Good. It's a deal then."

The Claiborne wagon was about a block from their cabin when they saw an elderly Cherokee couple walking slowly along the side of the street. All three waved at them, and the couple waved back. A moment later, Cherokee Rose noticed her father wiping tears from his eyes.

"Father, what is wrong?" she said, leaning close.

Walugo sniffed and wiped more tears. "Oh, just seeing Kindo and his wife together made me think of your mother. I miss Naya so much. I…I cannot really wish her back because she has been in heaven with the Lord for so many years and this earth would be a dull place for her now…but I still miss her terribly."

Cherokee Rose blinked at her own tears. "I miss Mother very much, too." She squeezed Walugo's arm and said, "Father, it will not be very long until all of us will be in heaven together."

Walugo nodded. "You are right, sweet girl."

Cherokee Rose turned to her husband. "Britt, I can hardly wait to meet your parents."

Britt nodded and sniffed, finding tears welling up in his own eyes. "Oh, won't that be a wonderful day! After I kneel before my Saviour, then rise to my feet and hug Him, I want to hug my parents!"

All three in the Claiborne wagon were wiping tears as they pulled up to their cabin.

Their dinner had been slowly cooking since just before they left for church that morning. The fragrance of roast chicken and dressing met them when Britt opened the door.

As they were taking off their coats in the foyer, Cherokee Rose said, "You two just sit down in the parlor, and I will let you know when dinner is ready."

As Cherokee Rose headed for the kitchen, Walugo followed Britt into the parlor and sat down in an overstuffed chair close to the fireplace. Britt added logs to the fire, and in a few minutes, the fireplace was giving off plenty of heat.

Britt sat in an identical overstuffed chair next to Walugo, and they talked quietly about the pastor's sermon that morning. Before long, Britt noticed Walugo go quiet and that his head was bobbing forward and his eyes were drooping. He decided to let the old man snooze a little before dinnertime. Quietly, he left the room and went to the kitchen.

Cherokee Rose was taking pieces of roast chicken from a pan on the stove when Britt entered the kitchen. "Your father is napping. Anything I can do to help?"

She handed him a platter of roast chicken. "Thank you, honey. You can put this on the table for me, and then go wake Father up. Everything else is ready."

Britt carried the platter to the table, which was covered by a snowy-white cloth, then went to the parlor. Walugo was slouched on the chair, asleep.

Britt touched his bony shoulder and said, "Walugo…Walugo…"

The old man's head bobbed as his eyes opened and he focused on his son-in-law.

"Dinner is ready," Britt said softly. "Are you hungry?"

Walugo licked his lips and nodded. "Guess I am," he said.

Britt helped him from the chair, and Walugo ejected a slight gasp, putting a hand to his chest.

"Are you all right?" Britt asked.

Walugo gave him a faint smile. "I think so. Just a little pain in my chest. I will be right as rain after some of my daughter's roast chicken and dressing."

Britt walked beside his father-in-law on the way to the kitchen, a feeling of concern tugging at his mind.

four

uring Sunday dinner, Britt and Cherokee Rose Claiborne talked of how much they loved Pastor Joshudo and his wife, but this was mixed with how much they still missed Pastor Layne Ward and his wife, Sylvia, who were now in heaven. Walugo joined in the conversation a little, not wanting his daughter to know that he was feeling poorly.

As they talked, Cherokee Rose seemed unaware of her father's small appetite. Britt, however, noticed how the old man slowly pushed his food around on his plate, but little of it made its way to his mouth. The old man's usually ruddy features had paled some. Britt also noticed that from time to time Walugo massaged his chest when Cherokee Rose was looking the other way.

Cherokee Rose and her father discussed how Layne and Sylvia Ward had worked among the North Carolina Cherokees when the United States government sent the army to escort the Cherokees to what was then known as Indian Territory. The Wards had voluntarily made the journey with them.

Cherokee Rose took hold of Britt's hand and said, "I am so glad you were one of those soldiers who was sent to escort us westward. Otherwise, we would never have met."

Britt smiled and squeezed her hand. "I've thanked the Lord for that countless times."

Tears misted Cherokee Rose's eyes. "I am so happy that the Lord chose us for each other."

Walugo wiped his own tears with a shaky hand. "God was so good to bring the two of you together."

Soon the meal was over, and rising from her chair, Cherokee Rose said, "You two go on back to the parlor. I'll bring you some coffee, and you can relax while I clean up. It won't take me but a few minutes, then we can go for our ride."

"I'll be glad to help you, sweetheart," Britt said.

"No, no, I'll be fine. You just keep my sweet father company."

The two men did as they were told, and shortly after they had sat down in front of the fireplace on the overstuffed chairs, Cherokee Rose entered the parlor carrying a tray. She placed two steaming cups of coffee on the small table between them, then bustled out of the room in her usual energetic manner. Both men smiled as they watched her depart.

"Walugo, I noticed that you ate very little today," Britt said. "And I saw you rubbing your chest when Cherokee Rose wasn't looking. I think I'd better go for one of the doctors here in town."

Walugo turned his dim eyes toward the man who was just like a son to him. "No need to get a doctor, Britt. The pains have stopped. I am an old man and full of days now. I know it will not be too long until I go to my 'long home.' People my age have pains in one place or another quite frequently. I do not want my daughter to know about these pains I have had today. It will just worry her. You know Cherokee Rose. She would just fuss over me endlessly and wear herself out. I sure do not want that! I get a little short of breath now and then, but I have been in God's hands for so many, many years. He will keep me here on earth until it is His time to take me to His Promised Land."

Britt gave him a thin smile. "All right. I won't say anything to that sweet lady that we both love so much. But don't be surprised if she picks up on it."

"You know, son, nothing that sweet lady does would surprise me, but let us keep it between us as long as we can."

Britt nodded. "If that is your desire, we'll keep it between us."

"Thank you."

When Cherokee Rose had finished her work in the kitchen, she went to the parlor and found Britt reading his Bible while Walugo was napping again. Britt got up to stoke the fire in the fireplace, and Walugo awakened and found his daughter standing over him with his coat in her hands.

Minutes later they left the cabin. Britt helped Cherokee Rose onto the wagon seat, then did the same for Walugo. Britt climbed up, took the reins in hand, and guided the horses southward out of Tahlequah.

When they were about two miles from the closest of the new Indian villages that had been established on reservation land, they met up with two Cherokee men on horseback. The two men pulled rein.

"How are things going in your village?" Britt asked.

Both Kinado and Flintini frowned, petulance showing on their dark faces.

"The last of the cabins out there in the fields in what was Cherokee farmland are being brought into the reservation village by the soldiers today," Flintini said.

"I hate the United States government, Chief Britt Claiborne!" Kinado said, his dark eyes blazing. "It gave our people this land and told them it would always be theirs. Now the president and his government have broken the promise and have taken the land away from us and are about to give it to the white intruders! Though Flintini and Kinado were born long after our parents and grandparents were forced to come west to Indian Territory, we still resent it. And so do many others. Flintini and Kinado are considering leading a rebellion against the government! We are sure that many Cherokees will follow us, as well as men from the other four tribes."

Cherokee Rose and her father exchanged apprehensive looks.

"If you and your men rebel against the United States government," Britt said, "you and your families will suffer for it. The rebellion will bring violence, and many Indians will die. The army units that President Harrison will send here will outnumber all the fighting men the five tribes can muster, and they have powerful weapons that the Indians do not have."

Kinado sat his horse, shoulders squared and jaw protruding. "Something else I resent, Chief Claiborne! I resent the Fort Gibson soldiers who are moving the Indians' cabins onto reservation land. Those soldiers should refuse to move the cabins! If they would do that, it would make it impossible for the Indians to be made to live in villages!"

"You're letting your anger control you, Kinado," Britt said. "I understand why you're angry, but you mustn't let it warp your good sense. Those soldiers are under strict orders from President Harrison, and besides, they're only trying to help, even as the soldiers of Fort Gibson helped build these cabins when your people were brought here a half century ago. Both of you men should show appreciation to the soldiers for the labor they're putting in to get the cabins moved. And even if they refused to move them, the government would tell you to do it yourselves or suffer the consequences. And believe me, those consequences would be severe."

Both Kinado and Flintini looked at Britt coldly, yanked the reins to the side, guided the horses past the Claiborne wagon, and rode away without another word.

Britt cupped his hands to his mouth and shouted, "I'm warning you not to rebel against the government! You and your families will suffer if you do!"

The two Cherokees put their horses to a gallop without looking back.

Britt sighed and put his own horses in motion. He drove

on toward the village without saying a word, and Cherokee Rose and Walugo remained silent.

When they rode into the village, they saw off to their right a log cabin on skids being put into place on the main street by army draft horses and two soldiers. Four Cherokee men whom Britt knew looked on with irritation showing on their faces.

Britt's attention was drawn to Dolfo, who was bigger and more muscular than the other three Cherokee men. Dolfo was shaking clenched fists at both of the soldiers, and suddenly he punched one of them on the jaw, knocking him down.

The other soldier reached for his rifle, which was in a leather rifle boot on the harness of one of the horses, but all four Cherokees grabbed him before he could get the rifle out of the boot.

A loud voice sliced the air. "Hey! Let go of that man and back off!"

The Indians turned to see Britt Claiborne climb out of his wagon and dash toward them. When they still held on to the soldier, Britt yelled, "I told you to let go of him!"

The Indians reluctantly released the soldier, but all four glared at the police chief, whose hand was resting on the handle of his holstered Colt .45 revolver.

Britt glanced to where the soldier who had been released was now helping his partner to his feet. He then fixed his attention on the muscular Cherokee and said, "Dolfo, why did you punch that soldier?"

"I punched him because I do not like white men," Dolfo said, his face flushed and his hands clenched at his sides. "Especially those who force us to leave our farms and move into the reservation villages!"

"That is correct, Chief Claiborne," another of the four said.

In the wagon, Cherokee Rose tried to climb down from the seat, but Walugo gripped her arm, saying she must let Britt handle the situation by himself. Cherokee Rose met her father's gaze, relaxed slightly, then looked back at her husband and the much younger and larger man he was facing.

Britt was trying to reason with the four Indians, saying that the soldiers were only doing what they had been ordered to do by their superiors.

Suddenly, Dolfo took a swing at the silver-haired police chief. Britt dodged the blow, took one step back, and said, "You'd better back off, Dolfo!"

But Dolfo came at him again.

Cherokee Rose jerked her arm free of her father's grip, hopped down from the wagon seat, and picked up a four-foot tree limb on the ground beside the wagon. She squared her jaw and headed for the husky Indian who was trying to strike her husband.

Britt dodged another blow and said, "Cool off, Dolfo!"

But the anger-blinded Indian came at him again, fists pumping. His left fist shot out, but Britt went under the punch and smashed him with a powerful right cross to the jaw. The blow staggered Dolfo backward a few steps, and Britt followed him, determined to bring the fight to a quick end. He closed in fast, just as Dolfo was regaining his balance, and hit him with a left hook that snapped his head back and then drove a powerful right into his midsection. Dolfo doubled over, then Britt cracked him with a blow to the jaw that sounded like an ax striking a log. Dolfo's feet left the ground, and he landed on his back, out cold.

The soldiers and the other three Cherokees stood gawking at what they had just seen.

Rubbing his right fist, Britt turned and noticed his wife standing there, breathing hard, the broken tree branch gripped firmly in her small hands. There was a fierce glint in her eyes.

A grin split Britt's face as he realized what Cherokee Rose had planned to do. She took a good look at the unconscious Dolfo, then set her eyes on the other three Indians, who had not moved. Like the two soldiers, they were staring at the tree limb she held in her hands.

Britt took the limb from his wife's trembling hands and tossed it on the ground. He took hold of her hands, looked into her eyes, and said, "From now on, I think I'll take you with me whenever there's a chance I'll have to do battle."

Cherokee Rose was trying to keep a sober face, but a smile forced its way onto her lips, and she ejected a tiny giggle. "Well, that might not be a bad idea. I may not be able to wield a gun, but I guarantee you, I can use a tree limb."

Arm in arm, Britt and Cherokee Rose moved back to their wagon, where Walugo still sat on the seat.

Walugo looked at Britt and said, "I tried to stop her, son, but she would have none of it."

"Well, all's well that ends well. If she had cracked Dolfo on the head with that limb, we might be burying him now." He looked down into his wife's dark brown eyes and smiled again. "Thank you for coming to rescue me."

"You are more than welcome," she said, her eyes twinkling.

The three Cherokee men approached Britt and told him they were sorry for the way they had acted. He was right. The soldiers were only doing what they had been ordered to do and were only trying to help them get their cabins to the village. All three asked for the police chief's forgiveness, which they were readily given, then they turned and apologized to the soldiers, who accepted the apology.

One of the soldiers then turned to Britt and said, "Chief Claiborne, you really put that big guy down! You must have the muscles of a horse in your arms!"

Britt gave him a tight grin, then turned to the three Indians and said, "Pick up your friend and carry him elsewhere. And when he regains consciousness, I want you to tell him that if he causes any more trouble, he'll be arrested and put in jail."

"Yes, sir," said one of the Indians, and they made their way to Dolfo.

As the Cherokee men were carrying their limp, unconscious friend away, Britt saw the village's chief, Degalado, coming toward him from between two cabins.

The chief, whom Britt knew well, was smiling.

five

herokee Rose, Walugo, the two soldiers, and Police Chief Britt Claiborne had their eyes fixed on a smiling Chief Degalado as he walked toward them. In his late forties, the chief was wearing his normal buckskins, plus a light wool jacket because of the chill in the air, and his usual full feathered headdress. He nodded at Cherokee Rose and the two soldiers, then set his dark eyes on Britt and said, "When the trouble between these two soldiers and my men first started, the woman who lives in one of the cabins I just passed sent her son to my cabin to tell me about it. I came with the boy in a hurry, and when I saw that you were there, Chief Claiborne, I decided to stay back and let you handle the situation. I knew with Dolfo there, it might turn into a fight."

Britt nodded.

Chief Degalado went on. "I watched with great interest as you tried to reason with the men, and then Dolfo tried to punch you and got knocked unconscious. I must admit that you surprised me in how you put Dolfo down. I am almost fifty years old, and I know fully that I do not possess the physical strength nor ability that I had when I was younger. You really amaze me for a man in his seventies."

Britt grinned.

"I commend you, Chief Claiborne, for the way you handled the situation. It was good to hear Dolfo's companions tell you that they had been wrong in their attitude toward the soldiers and to ask for your forgiveness and then to see them apologize to the soldiers."

"I was glad for that, too, Chief Degalado."

"I want you to know that I am in full agreement with what you said about the soldiers only doing what their superiors have commanded them to do." Chief Degalado paused and took a short breath. "Of course the Indians in Oklahoma District are having a hard time being put on reservations and losing the land they have farmed for over fifty years, and I cannot blame them…but you are right in what you have been trying to get the Indians to see. They and their families will suffer if they rebel against the United States government."

"Chief Degalado, I am so glad that you see the way it has

to be," Britt said. "If the Indians went into full rebellion, they would not stand a chance."

Degalado nodded and pushed the feathers of his headdress from his eyes, where the breeze was blowing them. "I must say, Chief Claiborne, that I wish I could change things for all the Indians in Oklahoma District and make it so they were not under white man's government, but it is not possible. I must say, though, that in spite of the United States government forcing us to live on the reservations, they have left the Indians of all five tribes sufficient farmland around the villages so they will still have plenty of crops."

Chief Degalado looked at Cherokee Rose, who stood a couple of steps from her husband, and gave her a warm smile. He then looked back at Britt and said, "You do realize, Chief Claiborne, that if you could not have handled Dolfo, you did have a backup. I saw your squaw with the tree limb!"

She smiled at him. "You are right, Chief Degalado. I would do most anything to protect those I love." She looked down at the broken tree limb where Britt had dropped it earlier, stooped, and picked it up. "You never know when this might come in handy," she said as she held it in a ready position.

While the Cherokee chief was chuckling, Britt said, "Well, Chief Degalado, Cherokee Rose, her father, and I must be going."

The chief glanced toward the wagon and lifted a hand in a friendly gesture to Walugo, who responded in the same manner.

The chief then turned to Britt. "I am going to have a talk with Dolfo. Perhaps he will listen to me about his troublesome attitude."

"I hope so," Britt said.

Chief Degalado turned and headed back toward his cabin, and Britt and Cherokee Rose headed toward their wagon. Britt glanced down at the broken tree limb still in her hand and said in a low voice, "I sure am glad you're on *my* side!"

Cherokee Rose gave her husband a gentle poke in the ribs with the tip of the limb and said, "That's where I will always be…right by your side."

Walugo looked on as Cherokee Rose placed the tree limb into the back of the wagon. He chuckled. "I see you really mean business about not knowing when that limb might come in handy."

"That's right, Father. So I'm taking it home with me."

Britt picked her up and placed her on the wagon seat, then he climbed up, took the reins in hand, and put the wagon in motion toward the center of the village.

Britt drove the wagon slowly so they could speak to people along the village street. They found that most of the Cherokees in the village had accepted the circumstance they had been placed in and were doing what they could to make the best of it.

Soon, Britt turned the wagon around, and as the afternoon sun was lowering toward the west, they headed back toward Tahlequah.

As the wagon rolled over the prairie, Walugo's head began to nod. Cherokee Rose put an arm around his bony shoulders and said, "Here, Father, lay your head on my shoulder."

The old man nodded, eyes drooping. "All right, sweet daughter, I will just do that."

Walugo's head had been on Cherokee Rose's shoulder less than two minutes when he fell asleep. His head remained there and he slept soundly until Britt guided the wagon into their yard and pulled rein at the front porch.

When the wagon came to a halt, Walugo groaned, then he roused, sat up, and rubbed his eyes. "Guess I must have dozed off," he said. "Seems like I do that a lot anymore."

"That is all right, Father," Cherokee Rose said. "You have worked hard all your life, and you have earned the right to get lots of rest."

When the three of them entered the cabin, Britt took their coats and hung them on the clothes tree in the foyer. Cherokee Rose was on her way toward the rear of the cabin when Britt noticed that Walugo was rubbing his chest, and his wrinkled face was looking drawn and tired. He laid a gentle hand on his father-in-law's shoulder. "Why don't you lie down in your room and have a nice nap? It would do you good."

A knowing look passed between the two men, and Walugo said, "I think I will just do that, Britt. I am very tired, and I am chilled to the bone."

"I'll go in with you and get a fire going in your stove."

Moments later, the two men entered Walugo's room, and Britt quickly built a fire in the stove.

Walugo thanked him, then stood by the stove, holding his hands over the rising heat. He looked back at his son-in-law and said, "I will get a little heat in my bones. Then I will lie down on the bed."

"If you're still asleep when it's time to go to church, we'll just go on without you."

"I should be awake by that time, son. Come and see about

me before it gets too close to time for us to leave."

"Will do," said Britt, moving to the door. "You get some rest now." With that, he closed the door, leaving Walugo standing at the stove.

After a few minutes of warming himself, Walugo made his way to the bed, unfolded a heavy blanket, and covered himself. As he lay there, Walugo's mind went over the events of the day. A smile curved his lips as he thought about his daughter and her willingness to go to battle for her husband. He could still picture her with the broken tree limb in her hands.

Abruptly, the face of his beloved Naya flashed on the screen of his mind. "Oh, my sweet Naya," he whispered, "what our daughter did today makes me think of how *you* would have done the same thing for me, or for any of your loved ones."

The smile still in place, the weary old man closed his eyes, tucked the heavy blanket up closer to his chin, and fell asleep.

The lingering brightness of the sunset lightened the sky above Tahlequah as Britt Claiborne helped his father-in-law onto the wagon seat where Cherokee Rose was already sitting.

Walugo settled on the seat and smiled at Britt. "Thank you for coming into my room before you two headed out the door. I was about to get up when I heard you talking about just letting me rest. Yes, I need rest, but I also need to be in the church service with my brothers and sisters in the Lord, and I need to hear my dear pastor preach."

"We understand, Father," said Cherokee Rose, patting his arm. "I'm glad you feel like going with us."

When the Claibornes and Walugo entered the front door of the church building, Pastor Joshudo and his wife were there in the vestibule to greet them. Britt and the pastor shook hands, Joshudo said, "I just heard how you were forced to take on big Dolfo this afternoon and how you put him down."

Britt's eyebrows arched. "Oh? Who told you about that?"

Joshudo named two soldiers from Fort Gibson who were regular attenders at the church and had just told him about it.

Britt frowned. "How did they know about it? They weren't there."

"They said that the two soldiers who *were* there had returned to the fort and told the story to other soldiers, and soon it was all over the fort."

Cherokee Rose squeezed her husband's arm, smiling up at him. "Darling, that story will soon be all over Oklahoma Territory. How many men could have overpowered Dolfo like you did? Especially men who are many pounds lighter than her?"

Britt grinned. "Uh-huh. And more than that, you mean who are as old as I am."

She shook her head. "I never said that."

"But you *thought* it."

Walugo nudged both of them with his hands. "We must move inside. It is almost time for the service to begin."

"Maybe I'll change my sermon this evening and preach on Methuselah!" the pastor said with a chuckle.

Early on Thursday morning, February 28, General Lloyd Caldwell came out of his office at Fort Gibson and told the corporal at the desk that he was leaving for Tahlequah to meet with Police Chief Britt Claiborne and Chief U.S. Marshal Robert Landon at Claiborne's office.

Caldwell moved out the door, and an army private was waiting there, having bridled and saddled the commandant's horse for him.

At the same time that General Caldwell was putting his horse to a trot toward Tahlequah, Britt Claiborne was strapping on his gun belt before leaving for his office. As he tightened the belt, Britt noticed the look of concern in his wife's eyes.

"Honey, what's wrong?"

She took hold of his hand. "Britt, I don't want you to ever have to fight again like you had to at Chief Degalado's village last Sunday. And…and I don't want you ever to have to use this gun again. You are seventy-one years old and should not be having to take on much younger men."

Britt hugged her and kissed the tip of her nose. "Sweetheart, I am fully aware that I must retire someday soon, but I cannot do that yet. I have a responsibility to uphold with the land rush coming, and the help I must give the army and the deputy U.S. marshals that will be here, if they need me."

"I understand that, darling, but you really need to be seriously thinking about stepping down."

Britt nodded. "We'll talk about it more later and pray about it together, too."

Cherokee Rose walked to the door with her husband. They kissed tenderly, then as he walked down the street toward his office, she wiped tears from her cheeks and said, "Dear Lord, please keep Your protective hand on my husband."

—◠—

Later that morning at police headquarters, Britt was sitting at his desk when Officer Najuno knocked on the door and said, "Chief, General Lloyd Caldwell is here."

Britt rose from his chair and started around the desk. "Please send him in, Najuno."

Seconds later the two friends shook hands, then sat down on overstuffed chairs, facing each other.

General Caldwell commended Britt for how he had handled the trouble at Chief Degalado's village the previous Sunday afternoon, then the conversation went to the upcoming land rush on April 22, which would be preceded by seven weeks of prospective settlers from many parts of the country entering the District to look over the land.

There was a knock on the office door once again, and Najuno opened the door and said, "Chief United States Marshal Robert Landon has arrived."

Both the general and the police chief jumped to their feet.

"Bring him in, Najuno," Chief Claiborne said.

six

hen Officer Najuno ushered Chief United States Marshal Robert Landon through the office door, Landon's hat and coat were in his left hand, and he wore a wide smile. He appeared to be in his midfifties. An even six feet in height, he was clad in a black suit and white shirt with black string tie. He also wore a black vest with his gold Chief U.S. Marshal badge conspicuously in sight. He was square-jawed and stoutly built.

Introductions were made, then Britt gestured toward three overstuffed chairs and said, "Come, Marshal Landon. Let's sit down so we can talk in comfort."

The three men sat, and for several minutes they discussed the history-making event that was coming up.

"I want to tell you gentlemen that as my two escorts and I rode down from Kansas City," Landon said, "we saw a great number of people in wagons and on horseback coming this way. When we asked where they were going, everyone we talked to informed us they were coming to the District and would be entering through the official entrance east of here. If this is any indication of what it's like in the other areas that surround Oklahoma District—and I believe that it is—a massive crowd is coming. This is really going to be something to see!"

"All that is entailed in preparing for the land rush, and the actual land rush itself, are going to be colossal events," Britt said.

"General Caldwell," Landon said, "have your soldiers staked out the land as ordered by President Harrison, marking off each 160-acre section?"

"Yes, sir, the job is done. My men drove long steel stakes deeply and solidly into the ground so that wild animals cannot harm them or move them…and any men who attempt to do so will find it very, very difficult. The land is ready for the settlers to inspect."

"Good! And how about the land for townships?"

"Yes, sir. The land has been surveyed and sectioned off for six-square-mile townships, as the president and Congress have stipulated. And thirty sections are now available where new towns can be established. There will be plenty more land for townships later. This will still leave the vast amount of land for white settlers and the land that has been allotted to the Indians for their reservations."

Landon sighed and said, "There's no doubt in my mind that Oklahoma District is going to grow rapidly, and I'm sure it will one day become a state."

The three men then discussed the newspaper articles from all over the country that indicated that railroad companies were preparing to lay track across Oklahoma District and that stores, banks, and medical clinics would soon be established.

"I'm glad for all of this," Britt said, "because at present, Tahlequah is the only town in the District with stores and a bank, and it now has two medical doctors who are partners in a clinic."

Caldwell then told Landon that troops from forts in Kansas, Missouri, Texas, Arkansas, and Colorado had all arrived in the past two days and were gathered at their appointed places, where the official entrances had been set up by the Fort Gibson soldiers.

The chief U.S. marshal was pleased to hear it. "The soldiers from these forts are already aware that at seven o'clock tomorrow morning, they are to gather on the south side of Tahlequah so I can meet with them. Of course, I want all the available soldiers from Fort Gibson to be there for the meeting, too, General Caldwell."

The general nodded. "I assure you that those soldiers who are not on regular patrol will be there—that is, except for the few who are still moving cabins for the Indians."

"You told me about plans for that project in the letter you sent me several weeks ago, General. Your men who cannot attend the meeting in the morning will have to be informed of all that goes on."

"I'll take care of that," Caldwell said.

"Marshal Landon," Britt said, "I want to assure you that during your stay here, my Cherokee police force will also be on hand to help the soldiers in any way they might be needed. And I am at your beck and call anytime."

Landon smiled. "I appreciate it, Chief. With so much going on, I may very well need help from you and your men."

The three men discussed other aspects of the big project until almost noon. Then they adjourned to the fort to eat lunch in the mess hall.

The sun was lowering toward the western horizon, painting the walls of the buildings in Tahlequah a golden hue that was slowly changing to red as Police Chief Britt Claiborne left the police building and started walking toward home.

Tahlequah's main street was unusually quiet as he made his way homeward. He was almost to the corner where he would turn onto the street that would lead him to their cabin just three blocks away and was unaware of a pair of eyes that watched him from between two buildings.

Suddenly, Britt heard the sound of hoofbeats pounding the soft surface of the dusty street, but the echoes of the sound made it difficult to determine where the hoofbeats were coming from.

Then suddenly, the galloping horse appeared, plunging from the alley between two buildings he had just passed. The rider swerved the horse toward Britt, who leaped out of the horse's path as rider and horse thundered past him.

The rider skidded the horse to a stop, reined it around quickly, and put it to a gallop toward Britt again.

Britt let the horse get close to him, then sidestepped the charging animal and reached up and yanked Dolfo from the horse's back.

Dolfo hit the ground hard in Britt's grip, but managed to squirm loose and jump to his feet. Britt could make out the purple bruises on Dolfo's face from their previous fight.

"I am going to beat you to death, Claiborne!" the Indian hissed. "I will show you this time who has the best fists!" He charged as he spoke.

Britt planted his feet and unleashed a hard punch to Dolfo's mouth, staggering him backward. Britt closed in quickly and hit him again.

Dolfo staggered backward once more, but planted his feet and bolted toward the police chief, his fists pumping. Before he could land a punch, he took a solid blow to the jaw and another to his nose. He went down, blood spurting from his nose.

Standing over him, Britt felt an impulse to kick Dolfo in the ribs, but in all his fights as a soldier and a lawman, he had never used his feet on a man. He was not about to do so now.

Bent over and breathing hard, Britt said, "You are…under arrest, Dolfo…for attacking an officer of the law! Come on. Get up. You're going to jail."

Suddenly, Dolfo shot out a foot, striking Britt on the right thigh and dropping him to the ground. Dolfo rolled to his knees, gripping the knife he had just slipped from the sheath hidden beneath his buckskin coat.

Britt's right hand went for the gun on his hip.

The sound of two rapid gunshots pierced the air.

Dolfo jerked from the impact of the slugs and fell flat on his back into the dust of the street.

Still breathing hard, Britt looked around to see two of his Cherokee police officers, both holding smoking guns.

At the Claiborne cabin, Cherokee Rose left the kitchen, where she was keeping supper warm on the stove, and went to the front door to see if Britt was in sight.

Walugo was sitting in the parlor and saw her move past the parlor door. He grunted as he lifted himself out of the over-stuffed chair and shuffled into the hall. He stepped up behind his daughter as she peered through the front door window.

"He is late," she said. "I hope he gets here soon. Supper is more than ready."

"I sure want to hear all about his meeting today with the marshal and the general," Walugo said.

"Me, too," she said. "I—" She focused on the figure that abruptly came into view at the street corner. "Here he comes!"

Cherokee Rose opened the door, and she and her father stepped out onto the porch into the cool air.

Cherokee Rose noticed the droop in her husband's shoulders and the slowness of his pace. "Father, maybe all did not go well in the meeting today. Britt looks tired and dejected."

Walugo put an arm around his daughter as they waited for Britt to make it to the front porch.

Britt saw his wife and father-in-law on the porch, looking his way. His strength was so depleted that he felt as if he were walking against a heavy wind. He also had a splitting headache.

When Britt stepped into the yard, Cherokee Rose left her father on the porch and ran to her husband. "Darling," she said, "you look like you're about to drop. You don't look too happy either. Did something go wrong in the meeting today?"

Britt shook his head and cupped her face in his hands. "No, sweetheart. Nothing went wrong in the meeting. All is well with Marshal Landon and the plans for the land rush."

By this time, Walugo was off the porch and drew up to them. Both he and Cherokee Rose gave huge sighs of relief.

"We have been praying for you today, son," Walugo said. "So white man's government is prepared for this big undertaking?"

"Yes," Britt said. "But something bad happened on my way home. Did you hear those gunshots a few minutes ago?"

"Yes."

Britt then told his wife and father-in-law about Dolfo trying to run him down with his horse, and how they fought. He described how Dolfo had pulled his knife to kill him...and how two of his police officers had come along at that very moment and shot Dolfo, killing him.

Both father and daughter looked at Britt wide-eyed, and then Cherokee Rose said, "Praise the Lord that He sent those two officers to you just in the nick of time!"

Britt laid a hand on the shoulders of Cherokee Rose and Walugo. "Come on, you two, let's get inside. I'm tired and hungry!"

"I want to hear about the meeting," Walugo said as they headed toward the front door.

"I'll tell you all about it while we're eating."

When they stepped inside the cabin, Britt took a whiff of the delicious aroma coming from the kitchen and gave his wife a tender smile. "Smells like my favorite meal. Fried chicken, mashed potatoes, and gravy?"

"Mm-hmm."

"Let's go!"

While the two men washed up, Cherokee Rose put supper on the table. The three of them sat down, and Britt led them in giving thanks for the food and for the Lord's protection. Then the food was passed around, and soon all three plates were full.

Britt picked up one of the pieces of fried chicken on his plate, and just before he bit into it, Cherokee Rose said, "All right, darling, let's hear about the meeting."

"Daughter, dear," Walugo said with a smile, "give the man a chance to get some food in him. He has had a hard day, and he needs some nourishment."

Cherokee Rose's face flushed. "I am sorry, dear. Please go ahead and eat. I guess I can curb my curiosity for a few more minutes."

After consuming a good portion of his meal, Britt told his wife and father-in-law about the day's meeting with Chief U.S. Marshal Robert Landon and General Lloyd Caldwell.

When the meal was over and Britt had finished telling them about the meeting, Cherokee Rose reached across the corner of the table and took hold of her husband's hand. "Darling, this awful incident today with Dolfo trying to kill you…I can tell it has affected you. Once again you had to do battle with a man much younger than yourself, let alone much larger. I'm so thankful that the Lord sent those officers to save your life, but it still has taken a toll on you."

"It sure has," Walugo said. "Even I can see that."

"I know you feel a tremendous responsibility to be available these next several weeks for the land rush." She squeezed his hand. "Don't you think this incident today and how it has affected you may be God's way of telling you that you should retire very soon? I mean…there are always going to be more stubborn, lawbreaking men out there for you to deal with."

"It may very well be the Lord's way of showing me I must retire soon, but it will have to wait at least until after April 22."

She squeezed his hand again. "God will show you the exact time to retire, darling. Our lives are His to guide as He sees best. We will just keep close to Him and let Him lead us."

Britt lifted her hand to his lips and kissed it tenderly.

Early the next morning, Walugo awakened at the sound of his daughter and son-in-law moving about the cabin. He had not slept well. There had been pains in his chest during the night. When he arose from the bed, the pain hit him again, and he sat down on the side of the bed and massaged his chest gently.

When the pain eased, Walugo dressed and looked at his reflection in the mirror on the wall. He noted that his face was a wrinkled mask. At that moment, he heard familiar sounds from the kitchen and knew breakfast would soon be ready.

"I have no appetite at all," he said aloud to himself, "but I must not let my dear daughter suspect my discomfort."

Walugo made his way to the door of his room and paused as he took hold of the knob. He took a deep, painful breath, then slowly exhaled and opened the door. The aroma of sizzling bacon met his senses.

Gripping the doorknob, Walugo bowed his head and

closed his eyes. "Dear Lord, please give me just a little more time. I would like to see this land rush thing settled. My Cherokee people have had to deal with so much at the hands of the white men just in my lifetime. Please let this new adjustment somehow be a good thing for them. I am weary, Lord, and I am ready to go to my 'long home,' even if you call me before the land rush is settled. Your timing is always right. So I will be listening for Your voice to call me to my eternal Land of Promise whenever my time has come."

He took a shallow breath and said, "I praise You once again, dear God, for sending those missionaries to my people, and most of all for letting me hear the gospel. Thank You, Lord Jesus, for saving me and for saving some of those in my family. As you know, I am especially looking forward to meeting my sweet Naya in heaven."

Feeling a bit better, Walugo left his room and followed the scent of bacon, which had now been joined by the scent of biscuits and coffee.

seven

ust before seven o'clock that Friday morning, March 1, the large crowd of soldiers gathered at the south edge of Tahlequah. Most of them were in dark blue uniforms, but those from Missouri and Arkansas wore tan uniforms. Chief U.S. Marshal Robert Landon stood on an elevated grassy mound. Flanking him were General Lloyd Caldwell and Police Chief Britt Claiborne.

Some fourteen of Britt Claiborne's Cherokee police officers were at the crowd's edge, and Britt noticed several groups of Tahlequah citizens coming on the scene quietly. Most of them, of course, were Cherokee, but a few white people were among them. His gaze fastened on Cherokee Rose and Walugo, who were sided by Pastor Joshudo and his wife, Alanda.

Landon's attention went to the gathering of citizens, and Britt said, "Marshal Landon, do you have any objections if those residents of Tahlequah over there observe the meeting?"

"I assume there are no troublemakers among the Indians, Chief Claiborne," Landon said.

"No troublemakers in that group, sir. They've been allowed to live in town and haven't been forced to move onto a reservation. We'll have no problems with them."

"Good. Then I don't mind at all that they're here. It'll be good for them to hear what's being said."

Precisely at seven o'clock, Landon faced the crowd and introduced himself, General Caldwell, and Chief Claiborne, then welcomed all the soldiers who had come to Oklahoma District from the forts in the surrounding states. He reminded them that the military units would be posted at every official entrance along the Oklahoma District border later that very day. He wanted the soldiers at each entrance to make sure that the prospective settlers who came to the District over the next seven weeks understood that President Benjamin Harrison and Congress had been very benevolent to open up Oklahoma District to the white people while putting the Indians on reservations.

Landon said he wanted the soldiers to tell the settlers how rich and productive the soil is and that there is adequate rainfall and plenty of water for irrigation. Landon paused a few seconds for effect, then running his gaze over the faces of the soldiers, he said, "President Harrison wants you to tell every prospective settler that for them, Oklahoma District is the 'land of promise.'"

The soldiers looked around at each other, and they could be heard repeating the name, the land of promise.

Landon, Caldwell, and Claiborne noticed that in the crowd of Tahlequah Cherokees, there were murmurings and scowls. Landon turned to Britt with a questioning look on his face.

"You have to understand that this is an insult to the Cherokees," Britt said. "When the government forced them a half century ago to leave their homes and come to this land, it was to be *their* land of promise."

Britt's line of sight went to Cherokee Rose. She had slipped an arm around her father, who was weeping, and was whispering to him. Britt knew her words were words of comfort. No one noticed the tears in Britt Claiborne's eyes as Robert Landon went on addressing the soldiers.

At the spot where Cherokee Rose stood with her father, Walugo was wiping tears with one hand and rubbing his chest with the other.

Cherokee Rose kept her arm around him as she turned to the pastor and his wife and said, "Father is not feeling well. I am going to take him over there by those trees and sit him down."

Marshal Landon's voice carried on the air as Cherokee Rose helped her father to a stand of trees and sat him down on a log.

"Father, are you having pain in your chest again?"

Walugo met her gaze. "I...did not realize I was rubbing my chest. *Again*, you say?"

"Yes. *Again*."

"You have known that I have been having this pain?"

"You thought you were, as white men say, pulling the wool over my eyes. I have been aware of it for some time, Father. How is it now?"

"The pain is easing off."

"Good." Cherokee Rose looked back at the crowd, then turned her attention again to Walugo. "Oh, Father, I so hope in my heart that our people will live peaceably on their reservations. We Cherokees have never been a warlike, vindictive tribe, and my prayer is for peace among our people and the white men."

Walugo took a deep breath and let it out slowly. "I know that Britt has tried to help the Cherokees and the other tribes here in Oklahoma District to understand that they will only suffer if they go against white man's government. God has blessed him with much wisdom. I only hope that when he retires, his successor will be as wise."

Cherokee Rose saw tears once again coursing down her father's wrinkled cheeks. She took hold of a bony hand. "We have been promised many things by the white men, Father. They have kept some of their promises, but have betrayed us on most. However, the God you and I serve always has and always will keep the promises He makes. The apostle Paul wrote that all of God's promises in Jesus are yea and amen!"

Walugo smiled. "Your words are a comfort to my heart, sweet daughter. I remember Pastor Joshudo saying once that there is always a Scripture to deal with every phase of life. I have had such a full life, and I feel that I have accomplished many things for the Lord in the years that I have been a Christian. But I miss your mother so very much and—well, my thoughts any more are fixed on that far Promised Land." He put fingertips to his temples and closed his eyes. "There is a Scripture about the inheritance we Christians have reserved for us in heaven."

Cherokee Rose nodded. "Yes, Father. It is found in 1 Peter 1:3 and 4, and I have it memorized: 'Blessed be the God and Father of our Lord Jesus Christ, which according to his abundant mercy hath begotten us again unto a lively hope by the resurrection of Jesus Christ from the dead, to an inheritance incorruptible, and undefiled, and that fadeth not away, reserved in heaven for you.'"

"Yes, that is the one." Walugo looked tenderly into his daughter's eyes. "I must tell you that whenever God is ready for me to come to heaven where your mother is, I am ready to take hold of that inheritance that is reserved in heaven for me."

Cherokee Rose's eyes welled up with tears. She kissed her father's cheek and looked at him through those tears. "All in His time, Father. All in His time."

On the elevated grassy mound, Marshal Robert Landon continued with his instructions to the soldiers.

"Men, your officers will appoint you to escort the prospective settlers—one soldier per family—as they make their way over the land. You must explain to each family that at high noon on April 22, when the land rush begins, every man must have a wooden stake with his name carved on it. And at a clearly marked corner of the parcel of land he has chosen, he must be the first to drive his stake to lay claim to that piece of land."

Landon emphasized that the settlers would be allowed to enter Oklahoma District only from one of the official border entrances attended by the United States Army. Each man who had a wooden stake with his name carved on it would be given a numbered card and have his name recorded. Anyone who tried to lay claim to a piece of property but could not produce a card would be escorted out of Oklahoma District and would not be allowed to return.

"Listen close to this now, men," Landon said. "I want you to give a solemn warning to all prospective settlers: Any claim jumper—that is, any man daring to drive a stake where another man has already done so—will face severe punishment at the hands of the military and will lose the right to ever again lay claim to a piece of land in Oklahoma District."

Landon then gave the soldiers an opportunity to ask questions. Only a few did, and when the questions had been answered, the meeting was dismissed.

Britt was huddled in conversation with Landon and Caldwell as the crowd dispersed. The three-way conversation was interrupted when Abondo, one of Britt's police officers, drew up to the mound, a worried look on his face.

"What is it, Officer Abondo?" Britt said.

"I am sorry for interrupting, Chief, but I must talk to you. It is very important."

Britt looked at the marshal and the general. "Excuse me for a moment, please. I need to see what this is about." Britt took the officer a short distance away and again asked, "What is it?"

"Chief Claiborne, just after the meeting was dismissed, a few of the Tahlequah Cherokee men discovered that there were four Creek men at the fringe of the crowd. They asked the Creeks what they were doing here, and the Creeks told them that they had heard about the meeting and had come to see what the government official from Kansas City was going to say. I guess what they heard made them more angry than ever, and…and they were saying bad things about Chief U.S. Marshal Robert Landon."

Landon and Caldwell looked over at Britt, who said, "Go on, Abondo."

"The Cherokee men tried to calm the Creeks down, with one of them quoting your words that to resist the white man's government would only bring suffering to those who do. One of the Creeks at that point said that he would like to 'kill that Chief Marshal Landon.'"

Landon's face paled a bit, but before he could say anything, Abondo licked his lips, glanced at Landon, and continued.

"While this was going on, a couple of Cherokee women alerted us police officers. When all fourteen of us reached the spot, the Creeks were railing at the Cherokee men, agreeing that Marshal Landon should be killed. We quickly arrested the four Creeks and put them in handcuffs. The Cherokee men told us the whole story, which I have just related to you."

"I'm glad you have them in custody, Abondo," Britt said. "Where are they now?"

"The other officers have them facedown on the ground, waiting for you to come."

Britt turned to Landon and said, "I'm sorry, Marshal Landon, that you had to hear this, but you needn't let it bother you. They will never get a chance to do you any harm. I'll turn them over to Creek Chief Komochi, who is a hard-nosed leader. I'm sure he'll lock them up in the village jail at least for the time you are here."

Landon managed a weak smile. "Thank you, Chief."

"Chief Claiborne, do you need any army help?" General Lloyd Caldwell said.

Britt shook his head. "My men and I will handle it, General. But thank you for the offer."

When Britt arrived home late that afternoon, he told Cherokee Rose and Walugo about the incident that had taken place after they left the meeting.

"When we hauled those Creeks in a police wagon to their village and explained to Chief Komochi what had happened, he was furious. He immediately had them locked up in the village jail. Chief Komochi assured me that they would be kept there for good and wouldn't be a threat to anyone."

Cherokee Rose nodded. "I am glad Chief Komochi saw the wrong in what those four Creeks did."

Later, at supper, they discussed the morning meeting. Walugo brought up what President Benjamin Harrison had said about Oklahoma District being the land of promise for the white settlers. Looking across the table, he ran his gaze between Britt and Cherokee Rose and said, "For the most part, this 'land of promise' has been taken away from us Indians. But those of us who have Jesus in our hearts have the *real* Land of Promise ahead of us, and nobody can take it away from us...ever!"

"That is right," Cherokee Rose said. "And one day all three of us will be there together with Mother. But Father...I do not want you saying, like you said this morning, that it won't be long till you die and go to heaven. Let us just leave that in God's hands, to take care of in His own time."

Walugo gave his only child a weary smile. "You know, dear daughter, when a Christian reaches my age, he looks at the future differently than when he was younger. The Lord has been very good to me. Although I have suffered many disappointments and gone through many trials, still I have been so very blessed. And you and Britt are certainly on that list of blessings."

Britt and Cherokee Rose looked at each other and smiled.

Walugo took a short breath and let it out slowly. "But I am tired now, and my body and my mind are telling me so. At my age, you grow weary in the battle of life, and as a saved man, I can only look forward to the rest and peace that heaven holds for me."

Tears filmed Cherokee Rose's eyes, but she smiled at her father and said quietly, "I understand what you are saying, Father. I am nearing seventy, and I am beginning to feel a little that way myself." She paused, blinked at her tears, then wiped them from her eyes. "But I have to be honest with you. I want to keep you right here with me as long as possible, because I love you so much."

Walugo was now fighting his own tears. He reached out and patted her cheek.

"I agree with Cherokee Rose, Walugo," Britt said. "I want

to keep you with us for a long time yet. I'm so grateful to the Lord Jesus that He died for our sins and rose from the grave to save all who would put their faith in Him. I'm so glad that you and my dear wife and I heard the gospel and were drawn to Jesus by the Holy Spirit…and that we have all eternity to be together in the *real* Land of Promise."

Walugo's tears were now coursing down his wrinkled cheeks as he said, "First and foremost, when it comes my time to go to my heavenly Land of Promise, I am going to see the precious Lord Jesus. Then…I am going to see my precious Naya."

The three of them wiped tears as they talked about what a joy it would be to see the Lord and to meet the angels and all the saints who were so prominent in the Bible. And to be reunited with friends and loved ones.

"We have such a wonderful future in heaven!" Walugo said, all choked up.

Britt took hold of his wife's hand and his father-in-law's hand and said, "Let's pray together and thank the Lord for all of His blessings…past, present, and future!"

eight

The next morning, Saturday, March 2, 1889, the eastern sky was a rainbowlike display of colors. Prospective settlers began arriving at the official entrances of Oklahoma District's borders north, south, east, and west. For many, the very brilliance and captivating colors in the sky brought hope for their future.

At every entrance, the soldiers could see that all were eager to look the land over and pick out the 160 acres they liked best in preparation for land rush day, April 22. Most of the men were in covered wagons and had their families with them. Some men were alone, on horseback.

Just outside the entrance a few miles east of Tahlequah, Lee and Kathy Belden and their sons, Brent and Brian, were waiting in their wagon. It had been a long, tiring journey for the Belden family, although they knew it would have been a great deal longer and more tiring had the train engineer not given them a ride across Texas.

The boys were excited and more than ready to help their parents pick out their new farm.

Brian, the fidgety six-year-old, leaned up close behind his father and said, "Papa, when are they gonna let us get started? We've been waiting here for hours and hours."

Lee turned and looked at him over his shoulder. "Settle down, son. It hasn't been hours and hours, it just seems like it. We can't go in there and start looking at the land until the soldiers give us the go-ahead. There's plenty of land, and we'll get the section of land the Lord wants us to have. I know it's hard to wait when we've come this far, but all in good time, we'll be on our way."

Brian eased back and looked at his brother, who was running his gaze over all the wagons parked around them, taking in the sight of horses and people. Nine-year-old Brett looked excited and ready to go, too.

"Papa, there are a lot of people here and lots of loud voices," Brent said. "So be sure you listen hard for the soldiers to call us, okay?"

Lee grinned at him. "Okay, son, I will listen hard. But don't worry. We've prepared ourselves and waited a long time for this day to come. Believe me, I'm just as anxious to find our piece of land as you and Brian are."

Kathy smiled at her husband, excitement showing in her eyes. She grasped his hand and gave it a firm squeeze.

In the crowd a short distance from the Beldens were Will and Eooie Balter, their daughter, Martha Ackerman, and her three children, eight-year-old Angie, six-year-old Eddie, and four-year-old Elizabeth. Martha sat on the wagon seat with her parents, and the children were just behind them at the opening of the canvas top. The children listened as their mother and grandparents praised God together for giving them a safe journey.

Nearby were Craig and Gloria Parker, who were also thankful to the Lord for their safe journey.

Also in the crowd of prospective settlers were Alfred and Barbara Decker, Donald and Jennifer Wooley, and Gilbert Gerson, his wife, Corrie, and their fourteen-year-old daughter, Peggy.

Soon the soldiers began walking among the wagons, explaining to the people that a mounted soldier would escort each family or individual while they made their way over the Unassigned Lands in search of a place to make their home.

Some thirty minutes later, the soldiers mounted up and led the wagons and the riders on horseback into Oklahoma District, and the people scattered north, south, and west.

As the wagons rumbled across the rolling prairie from every official entrance, many Indians, including women and children, looked on from their reservation villages.

Amid the numerous wagons headed due west from the

entrance east of Tahlequah were the Parkers and the Bakers. Though they were not acquainted with each other, they were driving their wagons side by side. The Ackerman children carefully studied the pair of mounted men in uniform who escorted the two wagons.

The first to catch sight of rooftops in the distance was six-year-old Eddie Ackerman. "Mama, look! A town!"

The soldier escorting the Baker wagon said, "That's Tahlequah, son. Right now, it's the only town in Oklahoma District."

Eddie looked at his grandfather. "Grandpa, could we pick out farmland that's close to the town?"

"Well, Eddie, we'll see."

"Looks like a real nice town," said Craig Parker, looking at Will from the adjacent wagon.

"And much larger than I had realized," Will said. "I'm thinking it might be good to pick out land not too far from it."

The wagons rolled on, and the closer they got to Tahlequah, all three Ackerman children became more excited. The Parkers heard Martha Ackerman and her parents talking excitedly as they pointed to the church building with the cross atop the steeple and the large sign just below it that said:

"GOD FORBID THAT I SHOULD GLORY,
SAVE IN THE CROSS OF OUR LORD JESUS CHRIST."

Craig and Gloria Parker heard the Bakers and Martha agreeing that they wanted to find land close by the town so they could go to church there.

"My wife and I are going to do the same thing!" Craig

hollered out. "A church that would put up a sign like that has to be one that preaches the gospel!"

Will smiled. "Yes, sir! You folks must be born again."

"We sure are."

"Us, too. Everyone in this wagon is, except the littlest girl back here. She's only four and not quite old enough to grasp sin and salvation yet."

The two families exchanged introductions and told each other where they were from.

Craig smiled and said, "If we can find two parcels of land that please us both, maybe we can be neighbors."

"Maybe so," Will said. "We'll just let the Lord guide us."

From his saddle, the soldier who was escorting the Parkers said, "I just happen to be born again myself, folks, and so is Corporal Evans, who is escorting the Bakers."

"Corporal Lundberg and I both appreciate that you folks want to find land close to Tahlequah so you can attend church there," Corporal Walter Evans said. "We'll guide you to nearby plots just a bit farther west of Tahlequah."

"Wonderful!" Craig said.

While the two wagons headed due west, Corporal Lundberg explained the procedures for making a claim.

"The reason for the stakes and the numbered cards is to keep claim jumpers from grabbing land illegally," Corporal Evans said.

"I like the way the government's handling this," Craig said to the soldiers.

"It's too bad they have to take precautions like you just mentioned, Corporal Evans," Will said. "But it seems there always have to be those who want to claim something illegally."

Evans nodded. "Sort of like Lucifer trying to take over heaven, and look what it got him."

"Isn't it great to belong to Jesus and know you're on the winning side?" Craig said.

"Amen to that!" Evans said.

The next morning at the Cherokee church in Tahlequah, Pastor Joshudo and Alanda stood at the front door and welcomed those who were coming for the services, including many strangers. Some of the visitors explained that they were prospective settlers. Among them were Craig and Gloria Parker, Will and Essie Baker, and Martha Ackerman and her children. Little four-year-old Elizabeth charmed Pastor Joshudo and Alanda with her sweet smile and big blue eyes.

Martha's children were guided to their Sunday school classes along with all the other children. Martha, her parents, and the Parkers thoroughly enjoyed the Sunday school class taught by a silver-haired man who was introduced by Pastor Joshudo as William Foster, the president of the Tahlequah Bank.

When Sunday school was over and the children were returning to the auditorium, many of the church members moved about, welcoming the visitors.

As the morning service began, a young Cherokee man directed the large choir, which was accompanied by a piano, and the singers for the special music were accompanied by a white man playing a violin and two Cherokee men on guitars.

When Pastor Joshudo stepped up to the pulpit to preach, he told the congregation that he knew that word had spread about Chief United States Marshal Robert Landon's statement that for the white settlers, Oklahoma District is the land of promise. Pastor Joshudo said that the Indians of Oklahoma District must live with what has happened to them, but for those who are born-again Christians, they have a far better Land of Promise to look forward to.

He asked the crowd to turn in their Bibles to the book of Hebrews, chapter 11, verse 9. He then read it to them as they followed along: "'By faith, he'—Abraham—'sojourned in the land of promise, as in a strange country, dwelling in tabernacles with Isaac and Jacob, the heirs with him of the same promise.'"

The pastor briefly described Abraham's journey into Canaan, which was God's earthly Land of Promise for him and his descendants.

"You see, my friends," Pastor Joshudo said, smiling as he ran his eyes over the crowd, "Canaan for Abraham was a clear picture of God's promise of heaven, which is *the Land of Promise* for all who put their faith in the Lord Jesus Christ to wash away their sins in His blood, to save them from hell, and to take them to heaven to be with Him forever."

There were many heads nodding and amens were heard across the auditorium.

After making the gospel clear, Pastor Joshudo gave the invitation, and several Cherokee people came to be saved. Christians in the crowd—both red and white—rejoiced.

When the service was dismissed, Pastor Joshudo and Alanda stood at the front door to speak to people as they were leaving. The Parkers, the Bakers, and Martha Ackerman and her children were in the long line. When they finally stepped up to the pastor and his wife, each one—except Elizabeth—

told their name and where they were from and said they were born-again Christians.

The pastor's eyes sparkled. "It is wonderful to hear that each of you know the Lord." He looked down at the little one and asked what her name was. She told him, then he patted the top of her head and said to the adults, "I am sure this little one will also open her heart to Jesus when she gets a little older."

Elizabeth smiled up at him, flashing her big blue eyes. "Mama says I will be able to understand when I am six years old. My brother and sister got saved when they were six."

The pastor nodded. "And I am sure you will, too, Elizabeth."

Alanda bent over, hugged the child, and kissed her cheek. "I was six years old when I took Jesus as my Saviour."

Elizabeth gave her a big smile. "Mama an' Grandpa an' Grandma told me that I am *safe* right now because I'm little. But when I get big and am six years old, then I can get *saved*."

"That is exactly right," Alanda said.

Craig and Will explained to Pastor Joshudo that they had looked the land over just west of Tahlequah and found property only a few miles away that they would like to claim on April 22.

Will said, "Pastor, yesterday, when we drove past Tahlequah, we saw the cross on top of your steeple, and when we read the sign with Galatians 6:14 on it, we wanted to live close enough so we could come to church here."

The pastor smiled. "Mr. Baker, we would love to have you in our church."

The Parkers, the Bakers, and Martha Ackerman said they

knew they were going to love being part of the church, then moved on so the other people in the line could talk to the pastor and his wife.

After a few minutes, Pastor Joshudo looked up and his eyes widened. "Chief Britt Claiborne, I did not do it!" he said, feigning fear. "Please do not arrest me!"

nine

olice Chief Britt Claiborne laughed at Pastor Joshudo's humor, as did Cherokee Rose and her father, who were at Britt's side. Alanda put a hand to her mouth and laughed, too.

Then Britt, who was eight inches taller than his pastor, leaned down and said, "I won't arrest you as long as you behave yourself, Pastor Joshudo. But if you ever preach against a man who's only a quarter Cherokee being the United Cherokee Nation chief of police, I *will* arrest you!" Then Britt said in a serious tone, "Pastor, I really loved your sermon."

"So did I," Walugo said. "It was wonderful. It really helped me a lot."

The pastor met the old man's gaze. "I am glad it helped you, Walugo."

The old man wiped a shaky hand across his mouth. "Since I am in my nineties, it will not be long until I go to the *real* Land of Promise."

Britt saw his wife's features tighten at her father's mention of his coming death. He squeezed her hand and looked into her eyes with compassion.

Pastor Joshudo laid a hand on Walugo's shoulder and smiled. "Just because you are ninety-one years old does not necessarily mean you will leave this world soon. You may live to be a hundred and ten!"

Walugo gave him a big smile. "If God wills it, fine, Pastor. But if not, I will be in my long home with Naya, whom I miss terribly."

Pastor Joshudo squeezed his angular shoulder and said softly, "I understand, dear friend. I understand."

"I do too, Walugo," Alanda said.

Walugo ran his eyes between them. "Just try to imagine what it would be like if one of you died, leaving the other one behind, and you will understand even better."

Alanda glanced at her husband. "That is exactly what I was doing, Walugo."

Walugo chuckled. "Then you *do* understand better already."

Britt led Cherokee Rose and her father out the door, and they stopped and spoke to several people as they made their way to the Claiborne wagon. As Britt guided the wagon team along the dusty street through Tahlequah, Walugo saw his daughter using her handkerchief to dab at the tears spilling from her eyes.

"What is wrong, sweet girl?" the old man asked, taking hold of her free hand.

Cherokee Rose sniffed, dabbed at her eyes some more, then turned to look at him. "Oh, Father, it is just so hard for me when you talk about dying."

"I am sorry, honey. I did not mean to upset you. I was not thinking clearly, was I?"

She only looked at him through her tears.

"Please forgive me, sweet girl. I should not have done that. I know how it upsets you. I will not talk about my departure from earth in front of you anymore."

Cherokee Rose squeezed the hand that was holding hers and said with a quavering voice, "Father, I cannot blame you for wanting to be in heaven with Jesus…and with Mother. But because I love you so much, the thought of you being gone from here is not a pleasant one."

Britt looked past Cherokee Rose to Walugo again. "One thing for sure, Walugo. When we meet in heaven, we will never part again."

As the days went by that week, the soldiers escorted many prospective settlers across the land. Before the week was over, railroad officials, merchants, medical doctors, and bank officials from many parts of the country had come to look over the six-square-mile sections where towns were to be established under government authority.

There were multiplied dozens of covered wagons parked near each official entrance on the borders of Oklahoma District, as well as many tents. The soldiers were escorting the prospective settlers onto the land as rapidly as they could.

The weather was gradually warming up, and each day found the people who were camped near the official entrances all around Oklahoma District borders quite busy.

At the entrance due east of Tahlequah, the Lee Belden family, the Craig Parkers, and the Will Bakers—with Martha Ackerman and her three children—were camped close to the entrance, each family having picked out the 160 acres they would go for on April 22. The Alfred Deckers, the Donald Wooleys, and the Gilbert Gerson family were camped right next to them.

Day after day, the younger children ran about the open areas between the wagons, shouts of glee and laughter filling the air. They also found places where they could play games together. Occasionally a squabble would break out among them and have to be settled by the adults nearby.

On Friday, March 8, at the Belden wagon, Kathy was busy doing the laundry while her sons, Brent and Brian, played with a group of boys nearby. Lee was several wagons away, out of sight, helping a man repair a wheel on his wagon.

Bending over, Kathy scrubbed vigorously at the load of laundry in a large metal tub full of hot, sudsy water. She paused periodically to stand up straight, dry her hands on the apron she wore, and massage the small of her back.

At one point she spotted her two boys happily playing tag with two other boys. Suddenly, Brian tripped and fell, rolling in the dirt as his brother and the other two boys stood over him, laughing. With a sigh, Kathy started toward the boys, but Brian quickly jumped to his feet, brushed the dirt off his pants, and the four boys ran between two wagons and vanished from view.

Kathy put her hands on her hips and shook her head. "Another pair of pants to wash," she mumbled to herself. Then a smile curved her lips. "Oh well, Brian, you're only a kid once. You might as well have fun while you can. There are plenty of sobering responsibilities waiting for you when you grow up."

She went back to the tub and dipped her red, roughened hands into the soapy water. While scrubbing away, she let her gaze roam around the area and focused on several other women occupied with the same chore. She kept scrubbing while humming a tune she had learned when she was a child.

On the following Sunday, March 10, the morning sun was shining down from a clear blue sky. After breakfast, Essie Baker and her daughter, Martha Ackerman, were just finishing up washing the dishes while Angie, Eddie, and Elizabeth watched their grandfather water the horses.

As Martha dried the last dish and set it on the folding table, she looked up at the azure sky and said, "Oh, Mama, what a beautiful Sunday morning!"

"That it is," said Essie, smiling. "One thing I love about this part of the country is the brilliance of the springtime sky."

Martha gazed at the rolling prairie westward toward Tahlequah. She noticed the small buds beginning to form on the trees, and here and there a little green shoot had poked its way out of the rich earth. She told herself it would not be long until colorful flowers appeared.

Martha turned to her mother, who was packing the dishes in a cardboard box. "I haven't told you, Mama, but I brought along some seeds from our flower garden at home. We can plant them close to our house when we get one built and be reminded of home."

Essie smiled. "That was a good thing to do, dear, but we must remember that Oklahoma District is now our home."

"I know, Mama, and I'm grateful for it. But I just can't erase the memories of where I was born and grew up. It was in Wichita were I met and married Troy…and where our children were born. I—"

"I understand, honey," said Essie, tenderly taking hold of her daughter by the shoulders and looking into her eyes. "But now that we're finally here, I want this to be the place we call home. Remember 1 Peter 5:10? 'But the God of all grace, who hath called us unto his eternal glory by Christ Jesus, after that ye have suffered a while, make you perfect, stablish, strengthen, settle you.'"

Martha nodded. "Yes, Mama. A wonderful truth."

Essie smiled. "I emphasize the words *settle you*. Martha, I just want to be settled once and for all until I go to my heavenly home."

Martha kissed her mother's cheek, then looked back into her eyes. "I know what you mean. I'm more than ready to put down some roots in Oklahoma District. I think of all these poor Indians who've been uprooted again and again, and I know that having to be put on reservations is not what they would've chosen. But I hope they can find some peace and security, and I hope the government will be truthful to them from now on."

"Amen to that," Essie responded.

Less than an hour later, the Bakers, and Martha and her children, dressed in their Sunday best, climbed into their wagon as Craig and Gloria Parker drew up in their wagon.

"Everybody ready to go to church?" asked Craig, smiling.

"We sure are, Mr. Parker!" Angie said. "Eddie and Elizabeth and I love our Sunday school classes, and we love Pastor Joshudo's preaching, too!"

Close by, Gilbert Gerson was busy patching a rip in the canvas covering of the family wagon. Peggy was sitting on a small bench a few yards away, and Corrie stood behind her, braiding her hair.

Corrie and Peggy watched the Parker and Baker wagons roll westward toward Tahlequah. Fourteen-year-old Peggy sighed and said softly to her mother, "Mama, I wish I could go to church."

Corrie finished the last pigtail and laid a hand on her daughter's shoulder. "Sweetheart, I wish we *both* could go to church."

"Just because Papa doesn't want anything to do with going to church shouldn't mean that you and I can't go."

Mother and daughter were unaware that Gilbert had heard Peggy's words about wishing she could go to church, had left the wagon, and now stood right behind them, his eyes flashing. Corrie and Peggy jumped with a start as Gilbert snapped at them, "Neither one of you have any business goin' to church! You hear me? No business at all!"

Peggy stood up from the bench, and both mother and daughter turned around, eyes wide, fear showing on their faces.

"Goin' to church would be a waste of time because there ain't no God to worship, pray to, or sing songs about! I don't want to hear any more from either of you about goin' to church! Parkers and Bakers and Martha and them kids talk so much about God and Jesus Christ and are always prayin' over their food like it fell on their table right outta the sky. Only weak-minded fools believe in God, and they're doubly fools if they think Jesus Christ was God's virgin-born offspring!"

"Peggy, we need to go do some cleaning inside the wagon," Corrie said.

As they walked toward the wagon, Gilbert followed, stomping his feet to emphasize what he had just said. He went back to repairing the rip in the canvas, as his wife and daughter climbed inside the wagon to do their cleaning.

That evening, as the sun was lowering toward the horizon on the prairie, Corrie and Peggy watched from beside their wagon as the Parkers, the Bakers, and the Ackermans drove past the official entrance into Oklahoma District on their way to evening services at their church.

Corrie sighed deeply and said, "Honey, when you grow up and leave home and are out from under your father's authority, you can go to church and learn about God and His Son. When I was growing up, though my parents wouldn't let me go to church, I learned a few things from neighbors about God and the Bible, about His creating the universe, and about God's Son coming from heaven to be born as a human child with no human father. I knew, then, that Jesus' birth was a miracle."

"I wish Papa would let us have Christmas in our home like other people do," Peggy said. I just wish I could learn more about all of God's works."

Corrie nodded. "Maybe someday, even before you grow up and leave this home, God will make a way for you and me to go to church. I want with all of my heart to learn more about Him and His love."

"Maybe someday." Peggy took a deep breath and sighed. "I sure wish I could have a Bible to read right now."

"I wish we both could, honey, but your father will never allow that unless God does something to make a way for that to happen when He makes a way for us to go to church."

"Well, even though Papa thinks the universe came into existence on its own somehow, we both know that God created it. Since He has enough power to make a universe out of nothing, I believe He's powerful enough to change things so you and I can each have a Bible, and we can go to church together."

Corrie smiled. "Yes, He is. And you just hang on to that fact, Peggy."

"I will, Mama. I will."

ten

As the weeks passed, great numbers of prospective settlers gathered at the official entrances around Oklahoma District's borders and were escorted by the soldiers across the rolling plains and through the hills where the grass was losing its winter look and turning dark green.

Starting the first week of March, the army officers at each official entrance had used the telegraph system soldiers from Fort Gibson had set up in Oklahoma District during February to send reports daily to Chief United States Marshal Robert Landon, who was quartered at Fort Gibson. The reports advised Marshal Landon of the number of prospective settlers arriving at the official entrances.

By Thursday, April 18, hundreds of covered wagons were parked near the entrances, and great numbers of tents had been pitched there also.

During the following three nights, a number of men sneaked in on foot under cover of darkness and hid on the 160-acre parcels of land they wanted to claim for themselves. These men had read in newspapers across the country about the wooden stakes with the settlers' names carved on them that must be used to legally lay claim to the sections of land. However, Landon had withheld the information about the numbered identification cards that the soldiers at the official entrances would give to the men when they showed their wooden stakes.

On Monday morning, April 22, 1889, the very air seemed charged with excitement. It was a perfect spring day. The sky was a brilliant blue, with only a few white clouds drifting overhead.

At the area just outside the official entrance due east from Tahlequah, a soft breeze ruffled the green leaves of the trees. Happy children played about the wagons, laughing and whooping.

At the Belden wagon, Lee watered his horses and listened to the joyful sounds of the children. He found himself just as excited as they were. He thought about the section of land that he and Kathy had picked out a few miles west of Tahlequah. He hoped they would be able to drive their stake on that one, but even if someone beat them to it, there were many other places to choose from.

Amid all the sounds of happiness around him, Lee had a sober thought. What if I get sick and am unable to develop the land and improve on it as the government expects? He rubbed the back of his neck. Or what if I should die before the five years are up? What will happen to Kathy and the boys?

Lee glanced at Kathy, who was standing with a group of women a short distance away and laughing at something one of the women had said. Lee knew his wife was very happy with the prospect of living in Oklahoma District. His gaze wandered about, and he focused on Brent and Brian as they laughed and shouted while running about with some other boys.

Suddenly, Lee's frown disappeared and was replaced with a contented smile. "Lee Belden," he said aloud to himself, "you need to keep looking on the bright side. Don't give way to any more negative thoughts. Kathy and the boys deserve a fresh start in life, and they don't need you throwing cold water on it."

Lee took a deep breath and squared his shoulders. He gazed toward Oklahoma District to the west and took in the wide expanse of blue sky and the vast rolling hills. "It's going to be all right. I *will* develop the section of land we move onto, and the government will like what I've done with it five years from now. My family and I are going to be superbly happy here!"

Before eleven o'clock that morning, Chief U.S. Marshal Robert Landon had telegraph reports from the army officers in charge of all the official entrances, advising him of how many prospective settlers they had at their entrances. This told him they had some fifty thousand settlers, including their wives and children, waiting to enter Oklahoma District.

The soldiers made sure that every man who expected to lay claim to a 160-acre piece of land had a wooden stake with his name carved on it. When they were shown the stake, the man received a numbered identification card.

The atmosphere at the entrance just east of Tahlequah was charged with excitement. As it drew close to midday, the soldiers moved among the crowds, telling everyone to get in their wagons or on their horses and form lines, facing westward.

In the Baker wagon, Angie, Eddie, and Elizabeth could not sit still. Martha did what she could to keep them seated, but they just had to wiggle and jump up and down a bit. The same was true in the Belden wagon with Brent and Brian and in many other wagons that carried children.

Peggy Gerson sat between her parents on the seat of their wagon. "Papa…Mama…I sure hope we get that parcel of land you picked out. I really love that creek that winds its way across it."

"We'd never be short of irrigation water for our crops, that's for sure," Gilbert said.

Peggy smiled up at him. "That would really make you happy, wouldn't it, Papa?"

Gilbert favored her with one of his rare smiles. "Sure would, honey. Sure would."

Peggy considered saying that it would really make her happy if she could go to church, but thought better of it.

On the seat of the Decker wagon, Barbara clung to her

husband's arm, and Alfred smiled at her. "Well, sweetheart," he said, "we're just about home."

Barbara smiled back at him. "Yes, we're almost home!"

Just behind the Decker wagon, Donald Wooley had his arm around his wife, who was so excited she could hardly sit still. Jennifer planted a soft kiss on his cheek and said, "We'll be on our land pretty soon, honey!"

Donald smiled and nodded, then turned toward her and looked deeply into her eyes. "I hope you realize just how much hard work we have ahead of us. It isn't going to be easy."

His words subdued her enthusiasm slightly, and then a smile produced dimples in her cheeks. "You and I are used to hard work. Of course, we'll have a whole lot more land to farm now, but having a place of our own will be very satisfying. Yes, we have a cabin and a barn to build, but I know we can do it. Our children and grandchildren will come and visit us. We'll grow older and eventually die here, but we'll enjoy this new home until then. Oh, Don, I'm so excited about moving into Oklahoma District! We've got lots of living to do yet!"

Donald gripped both of his wife's hands and gave her an appreciative smile. "What would I ever do without you? You always know exactly what I need to hear. And you are so right. We *are* used to hard work. We can and we *will* make this our land of promise! I love you, sweetheart."

"And I love you," she said.

At that moment, the soldiers called out for the lines of wagons and riders on horseback to head for the entrance. When all the settlers had passed through the entrance and formed one wide line, facing due west, an army officer rode up to a spot to the right of the line. Every eye was on him as he took out his pocket watch, held it in his left palm, and gripped the Colt .45 revolver in his right hand.

"It is one minute and thirty seconds until noon!" he called out. "Get ready!"

When a minute had passed, the officer raised the gun, pointing the muzzle toward the sky.

"Thirty seconds!"

There was tension along the line. Some of the horses bobbed their heads and whinnied.

"Fifteen seconds…! Get ready…! Go!" he cried and fired the gun.

Horse teams charged forward, stirring up dust with the wagons bouncing behind them, and saddle horses at a gallop stirred up dust of their own.

When Craig and Gloria Parker were nearing the 160-acre piece of land they had picked out back in early March, she scooted up next to him and took hold of his arm. "We're almost there, honey!"

"Yeah!" Craig said, shaking the reins to speed the horses up a bit. "We'll go straight to the spot the soldiers showed us where the stake has to be driven. There are other wagons and a couple of men on horseback not too far behind us. If any of them have chosen the same piece of land, we'll beat them to it!"

When they went over the rise and headed for the designated spot, Craig leaned from the wagon seat and looked behind them to see just how close the other people were.

At the same instant, Gloria's line of sight fastened on the

place where Craig would have to drive his stake, and what she saw caused her shoulders to shake with an involuntary shiver. "Oh, Craig! Look!"

Craig's head came around quickly, and his eyes followed the direction she was looking. She was squeezing her hands together until the knuckles were shiny white as Craig focused on the man who was driving a wooden stake on the piece of land they had chosen, at the very spot the soldiers had designated. His back was toward them.

"Oh, no. Somebody beat us to it." The words fell from Craig's mouth like stones.

At the same time, he noted that no wagon was in sight, or even a saddle horse. "Gloria, that guy didn't come through any of the official entrances to get here. There's no way he could've made it this quick on foot. Well, if he didn't come through one of the official entrances, he won't have a numbered identification card."

Craig guided the team straight for the spot where the man was, and he finished driving the stake just as the Parker wagon rolled up to a stop. Hearing the sound of the wagon, he turned around and set his eyes on Craig and Gloria. He appeared to be in his midthirties. Holding his sledgehammer at his side, he smiled and said, "Sorry, folks. This parcel is taken."

Craig hopped off the wagon seat, stepped up to him, and looked around. "Where's your wagon?"

The smile faded quickly. "I don't have to tell you where my wagon is, mister. Like I said, this piece of land is taken. My stake is in the ground, as you can see. You'll find another choice section, I'm sure."

"Mind if I ask your name?" Craig asked.

The man shrugged his shoulders. "Clete Hobbs."

Craig took a step closer. "I'd like to see your numbered identification card, Mr. Hobbs."

"What're you talkin' about? I don't need no such card! My stake is down and that's it! Now get back in your wagon and move on!"

"If you don't have a card, you've driven that stake illegally. Pull it up now, and *you* move on."

Gloria's hands clenched on her lap as she saw Clete Hobbs jump at her husband, swinging the sledgehammer at his head. Craig avoided the hammer and smashed a left to the man's ribs, doubling him over. He followed with a right hook to the jaw. Hobbs staggered backward, dropping the sledgehammer, and just as he found his balance, Craig slammed a solid right to his temple. He hit the ground, flat on his back.

Gloria was off the wagon seat and rushed up to her husband's side.

While Hobbs was trying to clear his head, Craig dropped to his knees beside him and said to Gloria, "I'm taking this man to the authorities." Craig removed the man's belt and used it to bind his hands behind his back.

Leaving Hobbs there on the ground, Craig went to where he had driven his stake, pulled it up, and broke it into small pieces. Craig then went to the wagon, reached in over the tailgate for his stake, and hurried back to the designated spot. He picked up Hobbs's sledgehammer and used it to drive down his own stake.

Hobbs was still on the ground, looking dazed, as Gloria stepped up to her husband. "So, are you taking him to the soldiers at one of the official entrances?"

"No. He needs to face the chief U.S. marshal. Do you remember that first Sunday we went to church in Tahlequah that I pointed out the United Cherokee Nation police headquarters building?"

"Yes."

"Well, we're going to take Mr. Clete Hobbs there so the police can take him to the fort to face Marshal Landon. I'm going to put him in the back of the wagon, and I need you to drive so I can keep an eye on him."

Craig then moved to the spot where Hobbs still lay on the ground. "All right, get up, Mr. Hobbs. You're going to the police station in Tahlequah. The police will take you to Fort Gibson, where the chief U.S. marshal is staying. You're going to face him for coming into Oklahoma District illegally. I could tell the law that you tried to bash my head in with your sledgehammer, too, but the other charge will be sufficient. When they find that you don't have a numbered identification card, you'll be in real trouble."

Hobbs said nothing.

Craig took hold of the man's bound-up wrists and jerked him to his feet. Then Craig picked him up and placed him on the tailgate and told him to crawl inside the wagon.

Minutes later, Gloria was on the wagon seat, and her husband was inside the covered wagon with Clete Hobbs. She snapped the reins and guided the horses toward Tahlequah.

Inside the wagon, Clete Hobbs muttered angrily at Craig, saying, "You could at least let me go. You don't have to take me to the police."

Craig frowned at him. "You broke the law."

Hobbs gave him a hateful look.

Craig met his hot glare. "You knew about having to have the stake with your name carved on it. How come you didn't know about the numbered identification card you would be given at whatever official entrance you used, if you entered the District legally?"

"I read about the stake I needed in my hometown newspaper. But there sure wasn't anything said about this card you're talking about."

When Craig did not reply, Hobbs said pleadingly, "How about just letting me go?"

"No way. You broke the law, and you're going to face the consequences."

"I'll get even with you, mister! Do you hear me? I'll make you pay for this!"

"That's going to be a bit difficult, Clete."

"Oh, yeah? How come?"

"Because from what I've been told, anybody who gets caught sneaking into the District to claim land illegally is going to end up behind bars."

Hobbs looked at him with fear in his eyes, then fell silent the rest of the way into Tahlequah.

When Gloria drove the wagon up to the hitch rail, Craig hopped down over the tailgate, then helped Hobbs as he made his way to the ground. Craig guided Hobbs into the office of police headquarters with Gloria at his side, and the young officer at the desk looked at Craig and said, "I am Officer Najuno. What is this all about?"

Craig introduced his wife and himself to Officer Najuno, then told him the story. Najuno said he would go tell the chief of police about it.

Moments later, when Najuno came into the outer office with Chief Britt Claiborne beside him, Craig and Gloria smiled, showing their surprise.

"My wife and I have seen you at church every time we've visited there," Craig said, "and we knew by your uniform and the revolver on your waist that you were a police officer. But we didn't know you were the *chief*!"

Britt told him how long he had been chief of police, then explained that Officer Najuno had given him only a brief explanation of what had happened. He asked Craig for the full details.

Craig then told Chief Claiborne the story in detail, leaving out how Hobbs had tried to hit him with the sledgehammer.

When Britt had heard the story, he told Hobbs that he was under arrest and would have to face Chief U.S. Marshal Robert Landon at Fort Gibson. Britt then told Craig and Gloria that he would need them to come along so they could tell the story to Marshal Landon.

"Chief Claiborne, you can ride along in our wagon if you wish," Craig said. "I'll drive you to the fort."

"That will be fine," Britt said.

With Gloria at the reins again, Craig and the chief of police forced the prisoner inside the wagon, then climbed in with him.

As the wagon began to roll toward Fort Gibson, Britt Claiborne looked at Craig and said, "I want to thank you for subduing this lawbreaker and bringing him to me. I suspect this kind of thing will happen many times during the land rush."

"I'm sure you're right, Chief," Craig said. "Seems like

there's always somebody who wants to grab something for free, but when restrictions are laid down in order for it to happen, they want to avoid them."

Britt grinned. "Isn't that the truth?"

eleven

n Creek territory of Oklahoma District, Chief Komochi stepped out of his cabin, which was on the main path through his village, and glanced up at the deep blue sky. He noted a gathering of puffy white clouds drifting along at the pleasure of a high breeze. The clouds were forming into what appeared to be a pair of horse heads looking down at him.

Suddenly Chief Komochi's attention was drawn to an elderly Creek couple in front of their cabin. The old man, Rebardi, was laboring to hitch up their wagon to their mule team, and his wife, Lennana, was trying to help him.

Komochi hurried to the couple, and as he drew up, he said, "Here, let me hitch the mules to the wagon for you."

Rebardi sighed and said, "Chief, that would be very much appreciated. We want to go for a drive and visit some of our Creek friends in Chief Ignando's village."

Komochi stepped up to hitch the wagon to the mules, and at the same instant, a male voice from behind him called out, "Chief Komochi! Chief Komochi!"

The chief turned to see a young Creek named Alusko, the keeper at the village jail, running toward him on the village's main path.

"Chief! Durko, Lenfini, Biskon, and Eduno broke out of the jail!"

Komochi's eyes widened as he thought of the four Creek men he had locked up a few weeks previously because they had threatened to kill Chief U.S. Marshal Robert Landon. "How did they get out?" he asked Alusko.

"I do not know for sure, but it appears they somehow picked the lock on their cell door."

The chief's face paled. "I must ride to Fort Gibson immediately and warn General Caldwell and Marshal Landon! I was about to hitch Rebardi and Lennana's wagon to their mules, Alusko. Would you do it, please? I must hurry!"

"Of course," Alusko said.

Less than ten minutes later, as Rebardi was about to help his wife into the wagon, they saw Chief Komochi riding his horse at a full gallop, heading northeast toward Fort Gibson. Chief Komochi also had his repeater rifle in the saddle boot.

At the same time that Police Chief Britt Claiborne and his prisoner, Clete Hobbs, were riding out of Tahlequah toward Fort Gibson inside the Parker wagon, the four Creek escapees were riding their horses northeastward toward Fort Gibson.

After breaking out of the jail, Durko, Lenfini, Biskon, and Eduno had dashed to their cabins in the nearby village. They grabbed their rifles, bridled their horses, and galloped away, leaving clouds of dust behind them.

They had no detailed plan yet on how they would kill Chief U.S. Marshal Robert Landon, but they had agreed that they must be patient. They would have to hide in the small forest just east of the fort's front gate, maybe even for a day or two, until they saw him come out of the fort. When he did, they would follow him and shoot him down.

Britt Claiborne hopped out of the back of the Parker wagon when they arrived at the front gate of Fort Gibson. The guards at the gate recognized the police chief and greeted him warmly.

"I have a prisoner inside the wagon who needs to face Marshal Landon," Britt said.

"Marshal Landon isn't in the fort right now, Chief Claiborne," one of the guards said. "There was a dispute this morning between two settlers over a parcel of land a few miles southwest of here. Both of them had arrived at that piece of ground at exactly the same moment, and both of them claimed their right to it."

Britt nodded. "I can imagine that this kind of thing will happen several times all over the District."

"Yes, sir," the guard said, "but at least the two men decided to settle their dispute peacefully. They both drove down their stakes so no one else would infringe on the property and came to the fort to talk to Marshal Landon about it. Intending to settle the dispute as fairly as possible, Marshal Landon felt he should go to the property and talk to them about it there. He took Deputy Marshal Randy Daggett with him."

"Is General Caldwell here?"

"Yes, sir. You should find him in his office."

"All right. May we drive the wagon into the fort?"

"Of course."

A few minutes later, Britt Claiborne, the Parkers, and Clete Hobbs, his hands still bound behind his back, sat before General Lloyd Caldwell in his office. Caldwell listened intently as Britt told him the story. At times, Britt asked Craig and Gloria to confirm his statements, which they gladly did.

The general glanced at Craig Parker, then fixed hard eyes on Clete Hobbs, who would not meet his gaze. "You're right, Chief Claiborne. This man must go to prison for what he did."

"General, when Marshal Landon returns," Britt said, "will you pass along what we've told you and ask him to come to police headquarters so he can decide the length of Hobbs's prison sentence?"

Caldwell nodded. "He should be back shortly. I'll inform him of the situation as soon as he returns."

"Thank you. I'll keep Hobbs in a cell at police headquarters until then."

Clete Hobbs's fiery eyes were unblinking as he fixed them on Craig Parker.

Craig met his stare and said, "Don't look at me like that, Clete. It's *your* fault you're going to prison!"

Hobbs started to say something, then licked his lips and remained silent.

As the four Creek Indians rode toward Fort Gibson with murder on their minds, they saw white families happily moving about their covered wagons where they had staked out their claims on the 160-acre parcels of land.

At one point, they found themselves approaching a spot some forty yards ahead where two white settlers were talking with two white men who wore badges on their chests.

Suddenly, Durko pulled rein and said to the others, "Pull up!"

The other three did so.

"Take a good look at the older of those two men wearing badges," Durko said, keeping his voice low.

Biskon's eyes bulged. "It is him!"

Durko quietly cocked his rifle and said in a half whisper, "Do the same! Be ready to use your guns! We will ride up quickly, shoot down Landon and his fellow lawman, and ride away!"

The other three cocked their rifles.

"Make sure that you put at least one bullet in Landon," Durko said. "We must kill him! And if we can, put a bullet in that other lawman so he can't shoot back at us."

Just as the four Creeks were about to put their horses to a gallop, they heard a sharp voice behind them. "Drop those rifles on the ground!"

All four hipped around on their horses, stunned to see Chief Komochi sitting his horse and holding his repeater rifle on them with the hammer cocked.

"I said drop those rifles or I will shoot you on the spot!" Komochi said.

All four rifles clattered to the ground.

The two lawmen and the two settlers had heard the chief's loud command, and when they looked that direction, they saw the chief holding a rifle on the four Creeks and saw them reluctantly let the rifles slip from their hands. The two lawmen moved that way slowly and cautiously, their right hands touching the handles of their revolvers.

"Get off your horses," Chief Komochi said to the escapees.

They immediately obeyed.

Komochi then left his saddle, keeping his weapon pointed in their direction, and stepped up close to them.

"Chief Komochi, why are you here?" Biskon said.

"I found out from Alusko that you had escaped from jail. I knew you would come this way to try to kill Marshal Landon. So…I followed you. When I came over that rise back there, I saw you sitting on your horses eyeing those four white men up ahead. And then I heard Durko say Landon's name."

They watched the chief U.S. marshal and his deputy draw up, and Komochi said, "Marshal Landon, I am Chief Komochi of the Creeks. These are the four Creeks who were arrested back in March because they had expressed their intent to kill you. They were brought to me by Police Chief Britt Claiborne and some of his men, and I locked them up in my jail."

Landon nodded. "Yes, I know about these four. Chief

Claiborne told me you had put them in jail, and I have expressed my appreciation to him for what he did." His brow furrowed. "What are they doing out of jail?"

"They escaped this morning. I rode this way because I felt sure they would head for Fort Gibson and try to find a way to kill you. Only moments ago, I rode up behind them and surprised them. Marshal Landon, they must be locked up in the Oklahoma District Prison."

"They will be," Landon said. "My business with those two settlers over there is finished. My deputy here is Randy Daggett. Randy and I will take them to Chief Claiborne, and he'll put them in the District Prison."

"Good," Chief Komochi said. "I would like to go with you so I can see them locked up."

Landon smiled. "Certainly. Chief Komochi, I want to express my deep appreciation to you for what you've done here, especially with men of your own tribe."

"When men have murder on their minds, they must be punished no matter who they are." Komochi's face went hard as flint as he met the fiery eyes of the four would-be killers. "It appears that they would like to murder *me* now."

"They won't get that chance, Chief," Landon said. "And thanks to you, they won't get the chance to murder me either."

As Craig and Gloria Parker drove their wagon eastward out of Tahlequah, Craig said, "Well, now that the Clete Hobbs ordeal is over, we can go claim our land and make sure no one else has the same idea that Hobbs did."

Gloria took hold of her husband's right arm. "There

always seems to be people who think they're above the law."

"Yep, you're right. This land is so very important to all of us new settlers. We certainly should be fair and honest with each other. No doubt some pieces of land are better than others, but what an amazing opportunity the government has opened up for all of us. Greed and selfishness are always ready to rear their ugly heads, but there's plenty of room for all of us if we work at this together peacefully and honestly."

Gloria squeezed his arm. "Let's get ourselves registered for that section where you drove the stake and head for home!"

Soon, Craig guided the wagon up to the spot by the entrance where a group of soldiers were talking. When they noted the approach of the wagon, the sergeant who had given Craig his identification card recognized him and stepped forward.

Craig pulled rein and waved his card at the sergeant. "I drove my stake on the section of land we want."

"All right, sir," said Sergeant Roy Hefton, taking the card in hand. "If I remember correctly, your name is Craig Parker and you're from Missouri."

"You remember right, Sergeant Hefton. I'm impressed."

The sergeant then looked at the card, noting the number and Craig's name on it, and handed it back to him. "I'll get on my horse and ride to the section with you so I can make a record of your claim, Mr. Parker."

"Fine," said Craig. "There's something I need to tell you about, first."

"Oh? What's that?"

Craig quickly told the sergeant about Clete Hobbs.

Sergeant Hefton nodded, with a solemn look on his face. "We've had six such cases reported here already today. Every one of those six men sneaked in at night as much as three days before the land rush officially began. We're holding them right now in that covered wagon right over there," he said, pointing with his chin. "At sundown, they'll be taken to Marshal Landon for sentencing. He'll no doubt have them put in the District Prison for a long time."

Later in the day, Police Chief Britt Claiborne was doing some paperwork at his desk when Officer Najuno tapped on the door and said, "Chief, Marshal Robert Landon is here with those four Creek Indians that had threatened to kill him. They escaped from the jail in Chief Komochi's village this morning, and from what I was just told, they were riding toward Fort Gibson. Chief Komochi chased them down and got the drop on them with his gun. He is outside, too, as well as Deputy U.S. Marshal Randy Daggett. Marshal Landon wants to see you about going with them to take the four Creeks to the District Prison."

Britt stepped outside and ran his gaze over the hate-filled faces of the four men on horseback with their hands tied behind their backs.

"Marshal, Najuno told me about these four escaping from jail this morning and how Chief Komochi caught up to them and recaptured them."

"That's right, Chief Claiborne," Landon said. "And I'd like for you, as chief of police, to go with us to the prison."

"Be glad to. I also have a prisoner to transport to the

prison. His name's Clete Hobbs, and I'll tell you his crime on the way."

"Okay. Get Hobbs and let's go."

Moments later, Britt came out of the building with Clete Hobbs in handcuffs. He put Hobbs on his horse in the saddle, then hopped up and sat behind him, taking the reins in hand.

The heads of the prisoners hung low as the group moved out of Tahlequah toward the Oklahoma District Prison.

twelve

s land rush day progressed, Chief United States Marshal Robert Landon was at the desk provided for him in his quarters at Fort Gibson. The telegraph transmitter was clicking rapidly, and Landon quickly translated the Morse code, writing the messages down.

After over an hour with messages coming steadily, a break came, and just as Landon was writing the last line of the most recent message, there was a knock at his door.

"Yes?" he called.

"It's General Caldwell," came the muffled voice from outside the door.

"Come in, General!"

The fort's commandant entered and noted the slips of paper with messages on them. "Looks like you've been a busy man."

"Sure have. What can I do for you, General?"

"Well, nothing really. I'm just curious what your deputies and the soldiers at the entrances are telling you about how things are going."

Landon gestured toward a nearby straight-backed chair. "Well, pull up a chair and sit down, General, and I'll tell you what's happening."

Caldwell picked up the chair and placed it in front of the desk so he and the marshal were facing each other.

"My men and your deputies have been sending messages for nearly an hour and a half, General. Many settlers have reported that they've encountered a number of men who sneaked into the District over the past two or three nights, but of course have no identification cards. Right now, at several of the entrances, they have these lawbreakers in custody."

Caldwell shook his head in disgust. "Looks like the Oklahoma District Prison is going to have some more guests."

"Yeah, more guests. I'm declaring these sneaks 'illegal claimants,' but I'm going to call them 'moonshiners' because they entered the District by the light of the moon."

Caldwell laughed. "Moonshiners, eh? Hey, that's good!"

Landon shrugged. "Well, the name fits them. In questioning these men, the soldiers and deputies have learned that they hid out in brush, forests, and ravines. Then when the land rush started at noon today, they already had their claims staked out. That is, until they were reported, and the soldiers and deputy marshals demanded that they produce their identification cards."

The general sighed. "Well, Marshal Landon, I hope our men have caught all the moonshiners. It'll be up to you to set their sentences for these crimes."

Landon matched the general's sigh. "I'll have to give it some thought. Justice certainly has to be served."

As the sun moved slowly across the wide, blue Oklahoma District sky, the spring day turned quite warm, but a gentle breeze kept the temperature comfortable.

Alfred Decker drove his covered wagon toward the section of land that he and Barbara had chosen early in March. While the wagon rocked and swayed along the way, Barbara took in all the sights as they moved westward. The grass on the rolling hillsides was now a dark green, and early wildflowers could be seen in many places in their bright, colorful arrays.

When the Deckers reached the 160-acre parcel they had chosen some six miles due west of Tahlequah, Alfred swung onto the land and said, "Well, sweetheart, here we are. No one has gotten ahead of us, so it's now ours!"

He pulled the wagon to a halt and quickly made his way down from the seat. He hurried around the wagon to help Barbara down, but she was already on the ground, twirling happily in a circle, her gingham dress billowing around her. She came to a stop in front of her smiling husband and threw her arms around his neck.

Alfred held her close. "This is it, darling! This is what we've been working toward and dreaming about!"

She eased back in his arms and looked toward the wagon. "Better get your stake and drive it in the ground right now!"

He kissed her cheek. "Yes, ma'am, I'll do that!"

Barbara watched him step to the rear of the wagon, take out the stake and a heavy hammer from his toolbox, and make his way to the spot where the stake was to be driven. She followed him, a broad smile lighting up her face.

Alfred stabbed the tip of the stake into the soft soil and drove it deep into the ground. Then he took Barbara by the hand.

"Let's take a walk. We need to pick out the spot where we want to build our house."

They had walked about a hundred yards when Barbara looked around at a grove of trees that cast a large shadow on the ground. "How about right here, honey? I'd like to have the house close to these trees."

"Looks like the perfect spot to me," he said.

"I'd like for the house to face east so the morning sun will shine on the front of it. I'll plant my garden on the south side. I can just visualize the house standing here right now, with the fence around the yard like we talked, and the barn will be back over there to the west. I can also see the crops growing lush and green out there in the fields around us." She hugged him once more. "Oh, darling, it was a hard decision to give up our home and come here...especially at our age. But I sure am happy to be here!"

"We did the right thing, honey. I just know it. First thing tomorrow morning, I'll cut some small limbs from those trees and make some stakes to outline the size and shape of the house. Then we'll buy some lumber from the Tahlequah Lumber Company and get started building!"

Barbara smiled up at the man who had been her husband

for almost forty-four years. "All of this work won't be easy, but it sure will be gratifying. Just think, our own place to call home here in the hills of Oklahoma District."

Will and Essie Baker, along with Martha Ackerman and her three children, were out of their wagon, standing on the 160-acre piece of land they had picked out in early March, just five miles due west of Tahlequah.

Will smiled and said, "Well, dear family, there've been times since we left Wichita that I wondered if we'd ever get to this place, but here it is, our 160 acres of hope and promise!" Will stretched out his arms and slowly turned in a circle, surveying the land.

"It's wonderful, Papa," Martha said. "A brand-new start in life, and I know we all are ready for that."

"Indeed we are!" Essie exclaimed. "We have a long road ahead of us to make this a fruitful farm, but with all of us working and pulling together, it can and *will* be done."

Six-year-old Eddie took hold of his grandmother's hand and smiled up at her. "I'll help, Grandma."

"I will, too!" said eight-year-old Angie.

"Me, too!" four-year-old Elizabeth said excitedly. "I like our new home!"

Moments later, the family watched as Will took his claim stake out of the wagon and began driving it into the ground. When he was about to finish, a man came along on his horse and drew rein.

"Hello! I'm your 'next-door' neighbor," the man said. "Name's Gene Vader."

Will struck the stake a final time, looked at Vader, and said, "Welcome, neighbor. My name's Will Baker." He pointed to his family. "This is my wife, Essie, our daughter, Martha Ackerman, and her three children, Angie, Eddie, and Elizabeth."

The sisters curtsied, and Eddie smiled, nodding.

"Where you from, Mr. Vader?" Will said.

"Durango, Colorado. Used to have a small farm just outside of town. Decided to come here and lay hold on a *big* farm."

"You have a family?"

Vader shook his head. "My wife and two children were killed four years ago, Mr. Baker, when they were traveling on a stagecoach in Arizona. They were on their way from Durango to visit my wife's parents in Phoenix. The stage was attacked by Apache Indians, and everyone on board was killed."

Tears misted Martha's eyes. She looked around at her three healthy children and silently thanked God that she still had them. Troy's face appeared in her mind, and a catch came to her throat.

"Mr. Vader, please accept my deepest condolences for the loss of your family," Martha said. "I am a widow myself."

Gene Vader made a thin smile. "Thank you, ma'am."

"Please accept the condolences of all of us, Mr. Vader," Essie said.

"Thank you."

"Then you're alone on your new property, Mr. Vader?" Martha said.

"Yes, ma'am, in the sense that no one's living with me. But I have the Lord with me at all times." He ran his gaze to Will and Essie, then back to Martha. "I don't know if you folks understand what being born again is, but it means that I've received the Lord Jesus Christ as my Saviour."

Martha's heart did a strange little skitter, and a warm flush stained her cheeks. "My parents and I are born again, and so are my two oldest children. My husband, Troy, is in heaven with Jesus right now!"

A smile brightened Gene Vader's features. "Well, praise the Lord! My wife and children no doubt have already met your husband, ma'am. How wonderful it's going to be to have Christians for neighbors. I can already tell that a warm friendship has been born right here."

In Tahlequah, Britt Claiborne left Officer Najuno in charge of the police station and jail and drove away in the family wagon with Cherokee Rose at his side. They had decided to take a drive and watch some of the settlers stake out their land claims.

Chief Komochi had just returned to his Creek village and found a small crowd gathered on the village's main path, talking about the jail break made by Durko, Lenfini, Biskon, and Eduno. In the crowd was Durko's older brother, Melakon. Though Melakon had not threatened to kill Chief U.S. Marshal Robert Landon, Komochi knew that Melakon was extremely angry over what the white man's government was doing to the Indians.

In Komochi's mind, Melakon was just one of thousands who felt deep anger toward the white government, but like the majority of the others had enough good sense to not rise up in rebellion.

"We have been wondering if you caught up with the four criminals, Chief Komochi," one of the middle-aged Creek men said.

The chief nodded. "I was able to catch them off guard and get the drop on them with my rifle. They were on their way to Fort Gibson to kill Marshal Landon. It so happened that Marshal Landon and one of his deputies were talking with two white settlers nearby, and Marshal Landon and his deputy helped me take the four criminals to Police Chief Britt Claiborne and from there to the District Prison."

"Chief Komochi, I cannot blame Durko, Lenfini, Biskon, and Eduno for feeling as they do," Bolimo, one of the Creek men, said. "The white man's government has mistreated us over and over for many years."

Some of the other men spoke their agreement.

"I understand how you feel," Komochi said, "but you remember what Police Chief Claiborne told all of us before the white settlers began to come into our land—that because white man's military power is greater than we could ever match, and white men vastly outnumber us, we would only suffer if we resisted their government. Do you remember him telling us this?"

"We well remember, Chief Komochi," Bolimo said, "and we agree that what Police Chief Britt Claiborne told us is right. We must obey white man's government or suffer the consequences."

Komochi ran his gaze over the faces of the men in the small crowd and said, "Please help me convince the rest of our people of this. I do not want any of them to suffer for resisting the white man's government."

The men nodded their assent, and as the chief walked away and the crowd dispersed, Melakon felt his hatred growing for Marshal Landon as the leader in taking the Indians' land away from them and forcing them to live on reservations. But he also felt a growing hatred toward the man whose name kept coming from Chief Komochi's lips: Police Chief Britt Claiborne.

Not far from where the Bakers, Martha Ackerman, and her children had staked out their 160-acre parcel, Craig and Gloria Parker were happily holding hands as they walked along the gurgling creek that ran across their property. Many trees lined both banks of the creek.

Gloria looked up at her husband, her face beaming. "Oh, Craig, I'm so glad that no one got ahead of us to claim this. It's such a beautiful piece of property. There are lots of trees on our land, but I especially love the creek and the trees that line its banks."

Craig smiled warmly. "I'm glad you're happy with our place, sweetheart."

Gloria pointed off to their right. "I think we should build our house on that grassy knoll over there. What do you think about that?"

"Funny…I was going to suggest the same thing. It's the perfect place for it. We can face the house toward the creek. It'll be just right!" Craig folded Gloria in his arms and kissed her tenderly. "I love you, sweetheart."

Gloria's eyes were shining as she looked into her husband's eyes. "And I love you. Thank you for bringing me to this beautiful place. It already feels like home to me!"

As they turned and headed back toward the wagon, Craig took hold of Gloria's hand again and squeezed it tightly. "I know we're going to be very happy here. Praise the Lord for His goodness to us!"

thirteen

raig and Gloria Parker were still holding hands as they walked back toward their covered wagon, which stood within a few yards of where Craig had driven the claim stake.

"I'm going to give the horses a drink," Craig said. "Why don't you sit down on that big rock in the shade of those two trees?"

Craig took the bucket from where it hung on the side of the wagon and walked the forty yards to the creek. After he'd given both horses a drink, he hung the bucket back in its place and was turning to walk to where his wife was sitting when he noticed a covered wagon coming from the west. As the wagon drew closer, Craig and Gloria saw that a man, a woman, and two small boys occupied the wagon seat.

"Oh, those are the people who passed us a little while ago, going westward," Gloria said. "I wonder why they're coming back so soon."

"Don't know, but I imagine we are about to find out," Craig said.

The wagon came to a halt a few feet away, and the driver hopped down and smiled as Craig and Gloria stepped toward him.

"Hello," he said. "My name's Lee Belden." He pointed to the three still on the seat. "This is my wife, Kathy, and our sons Brent and Brian."

"Glad to meet all of you. I'm Craig Parker and this is my wife, Gloria."

"Kathy and I noticed this piece of property a couple of weeks ago when we were looking the land over. We took note of it again when we drove past a little while ago."

"Well, Mr. Belden, if you liked this property so much," Craig said, "help me to understand why you didn't drive your stake down on it when you had the opportunity."

"Well, we spotted what we thought was an even better section of land a couple of miles farther west. This same creek flowed straight toward it, so we drove over there to take a look. We found that the creek doesn't run through it but veers off to the north about a mile and a half from here. We went ahead and looked at the land, but it wasn't as nice as this piece. So we came back here with hopes of staking a claim."

Craig and Gloria exchanged glances, then Craig said, "Mr.

Belden, we staked it out for the same reasons that you like it."
He the pointed to the grassy knoll. "See that small hill over
there? That's where we plan to build our house."

"Perfect spot for a house, for sure."

At that moment, a wagon came over a gentle rise from the
east and headed straight toward them. The team was moving
at a fast trot, and two people were on the seat. Craig and
Gloria quickly saw that Chief of Police Britt Claiborne was
holding the reins, and they recognized his wife from having
met her at church. Britt and Cherokee Rose both waved as
Britt brought the horses to a halt.

Gloria smiled at Cherokee Rose. "Just taking a drive?"

"Yes. We wanted to see a number of settlers laying claim to
their land."

Britt hopped down from the seat and then helped
Cherokee Rose down.

"Is that your stake over there?" said Britt, pointing.

"Yes," Craig said. "These folks are planning to drive a stake
somewhere around here, too. Here, let me introduce them to
you."

Lee Belden reached up, helped Kathy down from the seat,
and the boys hopped down behind her. The Beldens then
moved up beside the Parkers, and Craig introduced them to
the Claibornes.

Britt lifted his broad-brimmed hat, and the bright sun glis-
tened off of his thick silver hair. "It's a pleasure to meet you all."

Britt ran his gaze to the Parkers and said, "Even though
you've been coming to the church services, we don't know
where you're from. Maybe you could fill us in and tell us why
you came to Oklahoma District."

"We would like to know the same about you folks, too," Cherokee Rose said to the Beldens.

Lee smiled. "Sure. We'll let the Parkers go first."

Both the Claibornes and the Beldens listened intently as the Parkers told their story about Craig being sentenced to the Missouri State Prison for a crime he didn't commit, the loss of their farm while he was in prison, and why they decided to leave Joplin and come to Oklahoma District when he was proven innocent and released.

"That's some story," Lee Belden said. "My heart really goes out to you."

"I can certainly understand why you felt you could no longer stay there," Britt said. "Having been behind bars no doubt left a stigma on you in the eyes of many, even though you were proven innocent."

"It must have been awful to be in that prison, Mr. Parker," Brent said.

Craig met his gaze. "It sure was, son. Like a nightmare."

Britt looked at Lee and Kathy. "Well, tell us where you're from and why you're here."

"We're from Texas," Lee said. "The panhandle. We had a farm near Amarillo. We didn't experience anything quite like what the Parkers went through, but we did have a rough go."

Lee and Kathy then told the Claibornes and the Parkers of the devastating drought that destroyed their crops and led to the loss of their farm.

The Beldens went on to explain that they came to Oklahoma District to claim 160 acres of farmland because it was known for having plenty of rain in the spring, summer, and fall and plenty of snow in the winter.

"Having experienced severe drought, we especially wanted to claim a parcel of land with a creek running through it. We felt it would give us a sense of security, which we didn't have in the Texas panhandle."

Tears were streaming down Kathy's cheeks, and she wiped them away with the back of her hand.

Lee squeezed Kathy's shoulder tenderly, looked at the Claibornes and the Parkers, and said, "I hope you understand. Kathy has carried a pretty heavy load in all of this."

Kathy pulled a large handkerchief from her dress pocket, placed it over her face, and broke into sobs. Lee kept his hand on her shoulder, his own features showing the pain he felt for her.

Kathy removed the handkerchief from her face and ran her teary gaze to the Claibornes and the Parkers.

"I...I'm sorry."

She turned her back and walked a few steps away, trying to regain her composure.

Lee looked at the other couples. "She'll get herself under control here pretty soon."

Cherokee Rose and Gloria moved up beside Kathy Belden, and each put an arm around her. Kathy looked at Cherokee Rose, then at Gloria, wiped her tears with the handkerchief, and gave each of them a wan smile. "I'm sorry, ladies. I don't know what came over me. Please forgive me."

"Nothing to forgive," Cherokee Rose said softly. "I know what it is like to leave your cherished home and have to move someplace strange and new. When I was in my late teens, the United States government forced us Cherokees to leave our homeland in North Carolina. It was the only home I had ever known, and like all the other North Carolina Cherokees, I was devastated. I thought I would not be able to bear the heartache of it. As the weeks and months passed, I shed many tears. Over four thousand Cherokees died on the journey from North Carolina, including my dear mother."

Cherokee Rose sniffed and used her handkerchief to dab at a tear on her cheek. "But looking back on it, I can see God's hand in it all. In fact, it was on that awful Trail of Tears that I met Britt. He was one of the soldiers who accompanied us on the journey. But unlike most of the soldiers, he was kind and gentle, and he befriended me and my family. Britt and I fell in love, so I can see now that God used the journey to bring us together. We were married shortly after we arrived here."

"That's wonderful, Cherokee Rose," Gloria said. "The Lord does have a purpose for everything He allows to come into our lives."

Both of the younger women were looking with admiration at Cherokee Rose when they saw the Belden boys leave their father's side, rush toward their mother, and wrap their arms around her waist, tears in their eyes.

"Are you all right, Mama?" asked Brian, his chin quivering.

"We want you to be all right, Mama," Brent said.

"I'm fine, boys," Kathy said, patting their heads. "I promise."

The boys continued to scrutinize their mother's face, and seeing no further trace of tears or dismay, they each broke into a smile.

Kathy ran her gaze between Cherokee Rose and Gloria. "Thank you for your kindness toward me. You both have been a real help."

They smiled at her, each took a hand, and they walked her and the boys back to the men.

"Thank you, ladies, for being a comfort to Kathy," Lee said. "I appreciate it more than I can say."

"Well, both of us have had our share of heartache leaving our homes and coming here," Gloria said.

"That's right," Cherokee Rose said. "For me, it has been fifty years, but I will never forget what it was like to have to give up our homes and come to Indian Territory."

"Chief Claiborne…Mrs. Claiborne…" Craig Parker said, "I'd like to explain the disappointment the Beldens are feeling right now."

Britt and Cherokee Rose turned their attention to Craig as he told them about staking claim to this choice piece of land and of the Beldens coming back to claim it only to find that the Parkers already had.

Britt looked at the Beldens and said, "I hope you'll be able to find another piece of land with a creek running through it."

"I hope so, too, Chief Claiborne," Lee said. "As I said, the creek appealed to us so much because of the drought we went through back in Texas." He turned to Kathy and said, "Honey, let's park our wagon on the outskirts of Tahlequah this evening and buy some groceries at the general store there. We can start our search for another piece of land in the morning."

Kathy nodded. "Maybe there are still some sections left that have a creek running through at least part of them."

Gloria Parker turned and looked at Craig, and he could see in her eyes that her heart was touched for the Beldens.

He leaned close to her and whispered, "Sweetheart, though

this piece of land is everything we could ever want or need, I see an even greater need in the Belden family."

Gloria nodded her assent.

Craig took a deep breath and looked at Lee and Kathy. "Gloria and I just came to an agreement. We'll look for another piece of land and let you have this one. You folks have had too much sorrow already trying to succeed at farming with a lack of water."

Lee and Kathy looked at each other in amazement.

Lee cleared his throat, shook his head, and said, "We couldn't let you do that, Craig. This is *your* place. You've already claimed it. Thank you for your kind and most generous offer, but we'll find another place. You've already planned the spot where you're going to build your house. We just cannot let you do this."

"I've never known anyone with such big hearts," Kathy said. "Your offer means more than I could ever tell you, but Lee and I will find a good piece of land and just be happy to live here in Oklahoma District on a big farm and away from the drought. Thank you ever so much, but it just wouldn't be right." Her eyes were bright with tears.

Lee's voice showed the emotion he was feeling as he said, "I stand in agreement with Kathy, Craig. We can't let you do this."

Craig shook his head. "We won't feel right about this if you don't let us step aside and allow you to claim this property. We haven't had to battle drought, and we want you to know you have a creek running through your property. After today, with a great number of people driving down claim stakes, land like this just may not be available."

Lee and Kathy looked at each other. With tears misting his

eyes, Lee took hold of her hand and said, "Honey, look at the faces of these dear people. How can we refuse their offer? To do so would be rude and impolite."

Kathy nodded and said in a tight voice, "Lee and I so very much appreciate your kindness, generosity, and unselfishness. We…we will accept your offer."

Craig smiled. "Good!" He walked to the stake he had earlier driven into the ground, loosened it, and pulled it out. He hurried back to the others and said to the Beldens, "I'm glad I haven't yet gone to finalize our claim on this property. *You* can do that instead!"

Craig put his arm around Gloria's shoulder as they stood facing Lee and Kathy.

For a brief moment, there was silence. The only sound was that of the nearby creek, with its water gurgling as it followed its winding course across the property.

Finally, Lee and Kathy looked at each other and a smile passed between them. Then Kathy said, "How can we ever thank you properly? There aren't words enough." As she spoke, tears of joy bubbled up in her eyes and began to stream down her cheeks.

Gloria wrapped her arms around Kathy, and Lee shook Craig's hand.

After holding Kathy for a moment, Gloria eased back and said, "Craig and I want you and your family to find happiness in this beautiful land. Just let go of the past, with its hardships and bitter memories, and enjoy this place you can now call *home*."

Lee went to the rear of his wagon and took out his stake and a hammer. Everyone followed as he walked to the spot where Craig had just removed his stake.

As Lee was driving the stake into the ground, Britt leaned over and whispered to Cherokee Rose, "What a selfless attitude Craig and Gloria have. The Lord will bless them with a beautiful and fruitful place, I'm sure. You can't out give Him." Britt then shook hands with the Parkers, saying, "That was a mighty bighearted thing for you to do. I know the Lord will bless you for it. His Word says, 'Cast thy bread upon the waters: for thou shalt find it after many days.'"

The Parkers smiled and nodded.

"Craig and Gloria, this is a dream come true for us," Lee said. "Our appreciation knows no bounds. We will be forever grateful."

"Just be happy and enjoy your lives here," Gloria said.

"Craig…Gloria…Cherokee Rose and I will pray that the Lord will lead you to a choice piece of land, even though it might not have a creek running through it," Britt said.

"Thank you both," Craig said.

The Beldens exchanged glances at the police chief's mention of prayer, and a pleasant look formed on both their faces.

fourteen

 see you approve of prayer," Britt Claiborne said to Lee and Kathy Belden.

"Of course," Lee said.

"I'm glad for that." Britt turned back to the Parkers. "Like I said, I know the Lord will bless your unselfishness in giving up this choice piece of land to the Beldens."

"I'm sure He will," Craig said, "but we didn't do it for that reason. We did it because we believed it was the right thing to do."

"I don't doubt that for a moment." Britt paused and seemed to be pondering an idea. "I just thought of something. I know of a parcel of land a mile or so to the southwest of here. It has lots of trees and bushes, as well as plenty of farmland. Maybe it hasn't been claimed yet. I've got to head back to my office soon, but Cherokee Rose and I will take you there, if you'd like."

Craig and Gloria looked at each other and nodded, then Craig said, "We accept your invitation, Chief."

"Would you do us a favor?" Lee said to the Parkers. "Come by and let us know if that section you're going to have a look at works out. We'd like to know."

Craig nodded. "We'll do that." With that, he and Gloria headed toward their wagon.

Britt and Cherokee Rose had a few whispered words between them, then stepped up close to the Beldens. "Would you folks come to our church next Sunday? Our pastor is a full-blooded Cherokee, and he's a wonderful preacher. You would really enjoy hearing him."

Lee cleared his throat. "Well, I can't promise that we'll be there next Sunday, but we'll come sometime soon."

"You can't miss the church building," Britt said. "When you drive into town, the steeple with the cross on it is higher than anything else in Tahlequah. Sunday school is at ten o'clock, and the preaching service is at eleven."

"All right," Lee said with a smile. "We'll get there as soon as we can."

Some twenty minutes later, the Claiborne and Parker wagons came to a halt on the 160 acres of land Britt had in mind. He pointed to a spot on the ground and said, "Well, there's no claim stake there."

"Oh, honey, I really like this place," Gloria said, taking a panorama from the wagon seat. "It's beautiful!"

"If you want to ride in our wagon with us, we'll take you on a quick tour so you can get a good look at it," Britt said.

Soon the Parkers were on the seat of the Claiborne wagon with Cherokee Rose and Gloria sandwiched between their husbands. Britt put the horses to a steady trot and drove around the entire 160 acres so the Parkers could get a good look at it. There were many comments from the Parkers about the lay of the land, the patches of trees, the rich-looking soil, and the number of grassy knolls that dotted the acreage.

When they returned to the Parker wagon and Britt pulled rein, Gloria said, "Oh, I love it! It's a great piece of land. We won't have a creek, but other than that, we couldn't ask for anything better than this!"

All four left the wagon seat, and as they stood on the ground, Gloria said, "Craig, I know where I want our house to be built. That is, if it's all right with you."

Craig grinned and pointed to the nearest grassy knoll. "Right there, correct?"

"How did you guess?"

"That knoll is almost exactly the same size and shape as the knoll we picked out at the other place."

Her eyes were flashing with delight. "Okay?"

Craig put an arm around her shoulder. "Okay, that's where we'll build it, sweetheart. And right this minute, I'm driving our stake down!"

Gloria and the Claibornes watched as Craig went to the rear of his wagon, pulled out the stake and a heavy hammer, went to the designated spot, and began driving the stake into the ground.

After he hit the stake with a final blow, Gloria moved up beside him. The sun was just beginning to lower onto the western horizon, and a glorious sunset splashed the wide plains and rolling hills with color.

"Look, Craig," Gloria said, "it's like God is giving us His blessing."

Craig's face lit up with a smile. When the Parkers turned back to the Claibornes, Britt and Cherokee Rose were also smiling.

"Well, dear friends," Craig said, "Gloria and I will go to the entrance east of Tahlequah and make our claim official."

"Great!" Britt said. "And I'm going to say it one more time—the Lord is going to bless the two of you for your unselfishness. I mean, I believe He's going to bless you in a real big way."

Craig smiled. "Well, Chief, if He does, Gloria and I will see if we can share that blessing with you and this lovely lady standing beside you."

The sun had dropped out of sight when Britt and Cherokee Rose arrived home. Walugo had been sitting in the parlor, but was on his feet in the foyer when his daughter entered the front door.

"Hello, sweet girl," the old man said with a smile. "Did you and Britt get to see lots of people claiming land today?"

"Quite a few, Father," she said, kissing his cheek. "We will tell you some of the things that happened while we are eating supper. Right now, I must head for the kitchen and get things started."

Britt entered the back door of the cabin after taking the wagon and team to the barn. He spoke to Walugo, who was setting the table, then moved to the end of the cupboard where a wash pan and a bucket of water awaited him. After washing his hands, Britt sat down at the table with his father-in-law, and together they waited for Cherokee Rose to finish cooking the meal.

The food was on the table and Cherokee Rose had sat down to join the two men for the meal when there was a knock at the front door.

Britt scooted his chair back and stood up. "I'll see who it is."

Cherokee Rose and her father could hear a male voice speaking to Britt, but could not make out what was being said. A moment later, Britt returned to the kitchen.

"You two will have to eat without me, I'm afraid. Marshal Landon has called an important meeting at Fort Gibson, and as chief of police, I must attend. General Caldwell sent one of his soldiers to get me. I'll be back as soon as I can."

As darkness was falling on the plains, Chief United States Marshal Robert Landon stood before the large group of men who had gathered in the military assembly room at Fort Gibson. Several lanterns had been lit.

Present were a number of U.S. deputy marshals, some of the soldiers from the various forts in states around the District, a few Fort Gibson soldiers, including General Lloyd Caldwell, and Police Chief Britt Claiborne.

Landon ran his gaze over the faces before him and said, "Well, by now most of you know that we've arrested forty-five illegal claimants today, and they are locked up at the District Prison."

"Good!" one of the deputy marshals called out.

Landon smiled at him, then said, "Some of you know that earlier today I dubbed these illegal claimants moonshiners because they sneaked into the District by the light of the moon. Well, I'm now officially naming them sooners."

Landon noted the puzzled looks on the men's faces. "I'm naming them sooners because they entered the District *sooner* than the law-abiding settlers were allowed to enter." Landon then turned to Chief Claiborne. "We haven't been able to see each other today as I would've liked, but as chief of police, you need to know that while we were rounding up these sooners, thirteen of them resisted with firearms and were killed."

Britt nodded, his eyes widening.

"Adding those thirteen to the forty-five in the District Prison makes a total of fifty-eight who tried to claim land illegally today." Landon sighed. "Tomorrow, my deputy marshals will bury the thirteen dead ones wherever General Caldwell designates."

The general rose to his feet. "Sir, there's a small piece of land just inside the Oklahoma District border at the official entrance east of Tahlequah. The bodies can be buried there. I'll have one of my officers take your deputies and show them the spot."

Landon nodded. "Thank you, General."

⌐◦

As the meeting was going on at Fort Gibson, a lone rider made his way past the fort and into Tahlequah. A group of white children were playing at a corner on the main street, in the circle of light provided by a streetlamp. The rider pulled up near them, keeping his face in the shadows as much as possible, and asked if any of them knew where Police Chief Britt Claiborne lived.

A boy who looked to be about twelve years old stepped up and told the man on the horse how to find the Claiborne cabin.

As Melakon rode the direction the boy pointed, the hatred he felt toward the police chief was like a fire in his chest. He would have his revenge very soon.

At the Claiborne home, Cherokee Rose and her father were just beginning to eat their supper together. Walugo looked at Cherokee Rose, a momentary twinkle in his murky brown eyes, and said, "Daughter, this chicken and noodles and cornbread tastes every bit as good as it smells. And you make the best applesauce in all the world!"

Cherokee Rose smiled. "I am glad you like it, Father. Now let me see you clean up your plate."

They chatted together as the meal progressed, but Cherokee Rose was bothered by how little her father was eating. When he sighed and laid down his fork, she said, "Is that all you are going to eat?"

"I am sorry, sweet daughter, but that is all I can hold. If

you can save it, I will eat more for lunch tomorrow."

"Are you sure that is all you want? You hardly eat anything anymore, Father. Are you feeling all right?"

"Yes, I am all right. I do not want to worry you, but you see, I just cannot do much work anymore, so with such a small amount of energy going out of my body, I do not get very hungry."

"Well, all right. Would you like a piece of apple pie later?"

"I will have to see."

Cherokee Rose loaded a plate of food for Britt, covered it with a lid, and placed it in the warming oven. To her father, she said, "I know a man who will be plenty hungry when he gets home."

Walugo smiled as he rose from his chair. "That he will. If you do not mind, I think I will go sit in the chair in my room and rest."

"Of course, Father. I will check on you later and see if you want some pie."

Walugo planted a kiss on her cheek, then turned and slowly made his way through the house toward the hall that led to his room. Just as he turned into the hall, there was a knock at the front door. Walugo heard his daughter's rapid footsteps as she came from the kitchen. He leaned against the wall, listening to learn who might be visiting at that time of night.

In the foyer, Cherokee Rose paused to light the lantern on a small table near the front door. There was a second knock, and she called out "Coming!"

When she opened the door, she saw the face of a young Indian man she didn't know. She told herself he was Creek from his clothing and headband.

"I need to see Police Chief Britt Claiborne," the man said.

"My husband is in a meeting at Fort Gibson, and I do not know when he will be home."

Melakon grabbed Cherokee Rose and clamped a hand over her mouth. "I will just come in and wait for him!" He whipped a revolver from the holster on his waist. "I am going to put a gag on you. If you let out a sound, you will be sorry. I warn you, woman, if you give me any trouble, I will kill you just like I am going to kill your husband!"

In the hall, Walugo could hear every word that was spoken. He heard the man dragging his daughter down the hall and into the parlor. He quietly made his way to a closet in the hall where he knew Britt kept some firearms.

As he quietly opened the closet door, he heard the man shove his daughter onto the sofa, and he could hear her whimpering while the intruder tied a bandanna over her mouth.

fifteen

elakon stood over Cherokee Rose as she sat awkwardly on the sofa where he had pushed her. The bandanna wrapped around her head, covering her mouth, was so tight it felt like a coarse piece of rope.

He pointed the muzzle of his revolver between her eyes and hissed through his teeth, "You keep quiet, woman! I am warning you! Keep quiet!"

Cherokee Rose shivered as she looked past the black muzzle of the gun and met Melakon's hateful glare.

"Too bad your husband had to stick his nose in where it does not belong," Melakon said.

In her heart, Cherokee Rose was asking the Lord to do something to stop this man. Her silent prayer was so intense that it forced another whimper.

Melakon bent over her and pressed the muzzle against the bridge of her nose. "I told you to keep quiet!"

Suddenly, from behind him, Melakon heard a trembling voice say, "Back away from her and let the hammer down slowly. Then drop your gun, Creek, or you die!"

Melakon's head whipped around, and he saw an elderly Cherokee man holding a revolver with shaky hands. The gun was cocked and pointed at the center of his back.

"I told you to back away from my daughter," Walugo snapped. "Let the hammer down slowly and drop the gun! I will count to three. If you have not obeyed, this .45 caliber slug will rip through your heart! One…two…"

Melakon pointed his revolver downward, eased the hammer into place, then dropped it on the floor.

"Get your hands in the air!" Walugo said.

Cherokee Rose quickly left the sofa and picked up Melakon's gun.

"Get down on the floor and lie facedown!" Walugo said.

Melakon squared his jaw. But when he saw the determined look in the old man's eyes, he eased down on his knees, then went down on the floor.

"I want to know who you are and why you are here!" Walugo said, holding the gun in both hands, pointed at the Creek's head.

"I am not telling you anything."

Walugo pressed the muzzle of the cocked revolver against the back of Melakon's head. "I said I want to know who you are and why you are here!"

"All right! All right!"

On the dark street, Britt Claiborne sat in his saddle as his horse carried him toward his cabin. He sighed wearily and ran his hand over his face. *What a long day. And am I hungry! I can hardly wait to wash up and have some of my sweetie's good cooking.*

Britt drew close to his home and guided the horse up to the front porch. He was puzzled to see a strange horse with no saddle tied to one of the hitching posts. He quietly dismounted and tied his own horse to another hitching post, then stepped onto the porch.

He could hear two male voices inside. One voice was that of his father-in-law, and the other did not sound familiar. He could not make out the words, but the unfamiliar voice sounded agitated.

Britt pulled his revolver from its holster and quietly turned the knob to the front door. He quickly made his way down the hall toward the parlor door and heard his father-in-law say, "Well, you are not going to be killing my son-in-law, and you are not going to kill Marshal Landon either!"

Britt entered the parlor and saw Walugo bending over an Indian, who lay facedown on the floor with a revolver pressed against the back of his head.

"What's going on here?" Britt said.

Cherokee Rose hurried toward her husband. "This Creek came here to kill you, darling! He handled me roughly and tied a gag on my mouth. He did not know Father was in the house, and as you can see, Father came in and got the drop on him with one of your guns."

Britt stepped up to where the Creek lay on the floor. "Who is he and why did he come here to kill me?"

"His name is Melakon," Walugo said. "He is from Chief Komochi's village. Those four men from that village that you put in prison for threatening to kill Marshal Robert Landon…"

"Yes?"

"Melakon is Durko's brother. His plan was to kill you, as he put it, for sticking your nose in where it did not belong. And he was going to kill Marshal Landon for the same reason the others were planning to kill him."

Britt holstered his gun and took a pair of handcuffs off his belt. "Well, Melakon," he said as he knelt down beside him, "you can now join your brother and his pals in prison."

Walugo stepped aside as Britt began putting the cuffs on Melakon. Britt looked back over his shoulder at his wife and asked, "Did he hurt you, sweetheart?"

"No, not really," she replied, her voice a bit shaky, "but he would have if Father had not come to my rescue."

Britt locked the handcuffs in place on Melakon's wrists, then said to him, "If you had hurt my wife, you would've been sorry. You're in a great deal of trouble as it is."

Britt went to Cherokee Rose and caressed her cheek. He then looked back at his father-in-law. "Thank God you were here."

Walugo made a thin smile. "The Lord always provides for His own, son. He did not want my daughter hurt, and He did not want this Creek to kill you."

Walugo then turned and laid the gun on a small table. A

tight look of pain crossed his face, and he pressed a hand to his chest, though Britt and Cherokee Rose did not see it.

"I am going to take Melakon to the prison right now and see that he's locked up," Britt said. He nudged the Creek with his boot toe. "Get up."

A few minutes later, Cherokee Rose and her father stood on the front porch and watched Britt ride away into the night, leading Melakon's horse by the reins. Melakon sat glumly on his horse, his hands cuffed behind his back.

When they arrived at the prison, one of the night guards guided them into the cell block where Durko and his three friends were. They stared wide-eyed as the cuffs were removed from Melakon and he was locked in a cell adjacent to his brother's.

The next morning, Britt Claiborne was at the door of Chief U.S. Marshal Robert Landon's quarters at Fort Gibson and told him what had happened the night before.

Landon rubbed his jaw and said, "I've been considering making the prison sentence for Durko, Lenfini, Biskon, and Eduno ten years. I'll go ahead with that, but I'm going to sentence Melakon to twenty because of what he did last night in your home."

Britt nodded. "You're the man with the authority. He really made me angry for the way he treated my wife."

"I'm going to the prison right now to tell those Creeks the sentences I'm handing down."

"May I go with you?"

"I would welcome your presence."

—ᴄ⸱

When the chief U.S. marshal and the police chief reached the Oklahoma District Prison, Warden Yukindo welcomed them into his office. They sat down together, and Marshal Landon told the warden of the sentencing decisions he had made.

Yukindo nodded. "I hope these stiff sentences will convince all the tribes of the District never to rise up against the United States government, or against the law of Oklahoma District, as these men have done."

"I hope so, too," Landon said.

Warden Yukindo rose to his feet. "Well, my friends, let me take you to the cell block, and you can pronounce your sentences on them, Marshal Landon."

Moments later, the warden ushered Landon and Claiborne into the cell block where the Creeks were being held. Two husky Cherokee guards were with them. The prisoners in the surrounding cells looked on as each of the Creeks, who were sitting on their bunks, set eyes on the warden and the two men with him. Warden Yukindo told them to stand and step up to the bars.

The Creek prisoners eyed the two guards and stood up reluctantly, their faces solemn.

"Chief United States Marshal Robert Landon wants to address you," the warden said. "You are to remain silent and listen."

Landon went over the crimes that Durko, Lenfini, Biskon, and Eduno had committed, including their plan to kill him. Not one of them could look him in the eye. Landon then described what Melakon had done at the police chief's home.

"It was your intention to kill Chief Claiborne, am I right?" Landon said, looking at Melakon.

"Warden Yukindo just told us we are to remain silent," Melakon said.

Landon fixed him with cold eyes. "Then your silence convicts you."

The chief U.S. marshal ran his gaze over the faces of the other four and said, "I'm giving each of you a ten-year sentence in this prison for your crimes." He then looked at Melakon. "For the crime of going to the Claiborne home with the intention of murdering Chief Claiborne, forcing your way into the house when you learned from Mrs. Claiborne that he was not home, and treating her roughly, I am sentencing you to twenty years in this prison!

"You all had better be glad that you didn't carry out your murderous plans. If you had, you would be facing execution by a firing squad."

The next day—Wednesday, April 24—at the Belden place, each member of the family was busy. On this sunny spring morning, Brent and Brian were inside the covered wagon, putting new lines on their fishing poles. Lee was brushing his two horses in the shade of two cottonwood trees some thirty yards away. And Kathy hummed a nameless tune as she scrubbed the clothes in a galvanized washtub beside the wagon.

When she heard the sound of horses' hooves and the rattle of a wagon approaching, she looked up and saw Craig and Gloria Parker on the wagon seat.

Kathy dropped the wet clothes into the sudsy water and

dried her hands on her apron. Smiling brightly, she moved toward the Parkers as Craig drew the wagon to a halt.

"Good morning!" she called up to them. "Nice to see you. Won't you come down and stay a while?"

Craig hopped down from the wagon seat and helped Gloria down.

"I have some coffee staying hot over the cook-fire. Would you like some?" Kathy said. "Or would you rather have a nice cool drink from our babbling brook over there?"

At that moment, Lee came walking toward them, a smile on his face from ear to ear. He reached out and shook Lee's hand. "Hey, this is a pleasant surprise!"

Brent and Brian, each holding a fishing pole, hopped out of the rear of the Belden wagon.

"Howdy, boys!" Craig said. "How's the fishing?"

"We caught eleven yesterday, Mr. Parker," Brian said. "And me and Brent are about to go back to the creek and catch some more. Our mama makes the best fried fish in all the world!"

"Well then, I guess one of these days Gloria and I will just have to come for supper!"

Kathy's eyes lit up. "Oh, would you? Our accommodations aren't the fanciest, but you're more than welcome to have supper with us anytime."

"Thank you, ma'am," Craig said, bowing politely. "We just might do that."

"Good!" Kathy said. "We'll set a date and send the boys to the creek for an extra long time. Now, would you folks like coffee or some water?"

"Coffee sounds good to me," Craig said.

"Me, too," said Gloria.

Kathy took some cups from the wagon and headed toward the smoking fire a few yards away as Lee rolled some logs onto a grassy spot and invited the Parkers to sit down. Brent and Brian sat on logs close by, holding their fishing poles. Kathy returned with four steaming cups of coffee, and the four of them were seated on the logs.

"Do you happen to be here because you've found a suitable piece of property and have come to tell us about it?" Lee asked.

"Well, yes, that's partly why we're here," Craig said.

"So you found a good piece of land?"

"A very good one with rich soil."

"Does…does it have a creek running through it?" Kathy said.

"No, but it'll do just fine. We'll dig whatever wells we need to provide water."

Lee sipped coffee and said, "Kathy and I want to thank both of you again for your kindness and generosity in giving up this section of land for us."

Craig exchanged glances with Gloria, then smiled at both Lee and Kathy. "Our sacrifice was nothing compared to the sacrifice the Lord Jesus made for us at Calvary."

Lee and Kathy looked at Craig questioningly.

"I told you that the news about our new property is *partly* why we're here," Craig said. "The other reason we're here is to hopefully talk with you about what it means to be born again. That is, if you're willing to hear what we have to say."

Lee and Kathy nodded. Brent and Brian looked on, listening intently to the conversation.

Craig went on. "I heard you tell the chief that you'd come visit their church sometime."

"Yes, we intend to do that, and we do know who Jesus Christ is," Lee said. "He's the virgin-born Son of God."

"That's a good start," Craig said. "Do you mind if I go get my Bible? I'd like to show you some passages from the Scriptures that show us why Jesus came."

"Sure, that'd be fine," Lee said.

Craig hurried to the wagon and returned, sat down on the log, and opened his Bible. "Let me read to you from the Gospel of John what the Lord Jesus said to a man named Nicodemus, who was a ruler among the Jews: 'Verily, verily, I say unto thee, except a man be born again, he cannot see the kingdom of God.' The kingdom of God in this context is heaven."

"So unless a person gets born again, he cannot go to heaven?" Lee said.

"That's right. Jesus isn't talking, of course, about being born another time physically. Ephesians 2:1 says that we came into this world dead in trespasses and sins. That's spiritual death. So when we were born into this world from our mother's womb, we were already dead spiritually. That's why Jesus said we have to be born again. Unless we get born spiritually, we cannot go to heaven. The Bible is very clear on that. The Lord Jesus said so Himself."

"You see, when a person gets born again," Gloria said, "with that new spiritual life comes the forgiveness for all their sins. God will not let one sin into heaven. So if a person dies in their sins, they go to hell. If they die in Christ, they go to heaven."

"So how exactly does someone get born again?" Lee asked.

"In order to be born again, we must believe on Jesus' name," said Craig, flipping pages once more. "Let me read you

John 3:18. Of Jesus Christ, it says, 'He that believeth on him is not condemned: but he that believeth not is condemned already, because he hath not believed in the name of the only begotten Son of God.' To believe on His name is to believe that He is the one and only Saviour, who was sent from God to save guilty sinners from hell. To do that, He had to pay the price that God the Father demands for sin, and the Bible tells us that 'the wages of sin is death.' So Jesus had to die for sinners on the cross of Calvary. He paid the wages of sin. He also rose from the dead three days later and is alive to save us.

"To be saved—to be born again—we must receive Jesus into our heart. The Bible says, 'But as many as received him, to them gave he power to become the sons of God, even to them that believe on his name.' The Bible also says we must repent to be saved—we must acknowledge to God that we have sinned, that we are sorry we have sinned, and to turn from that sin and turn to Jesus. We are to call on Him and ask Him to save us and to come into our heart."

Brent moved toward Craig, eyes wide. "I want to call on Jesus to save me right now, Mr. Parker."

"Me, too!" said Brian, following his brother.

Both parents were ready also. Craig took Lee and the boys aside, while Gloria sat down with Kathy, and with the Parkers leading them, all four of the Beldens became born-again children of God.

From the Bible, Craig then showed the new converts that their first step of obedience to God was to be baptized. He assured them that Pastor Joshudo would be most happy to baptize them on Sunday. Lee Belden spoke for his family and himself when he said they would be there.

sixteen

t was early in the morning the next day when the soldiers stationed at the entrance to Oklahoma District due east of Tahlequah sat by the cook-fires finishing their breakfast. The sun had already tipped the eastern horizon a rosy red, and all the open land lay fresh and colorful in the morning light.

One of the soldiers stood and looked due south, then called to the lieutenant who was in charge, "Lieutenant Pitkin, I see a covered wagon coming this way."

The lieutenant finished the coffee in his tin cup and stood as other soldiers walked toward him, keeping their eyes on the wagon. When the wagon drew up, the soldiers saw two middle-aged men on the driver's seat and two middle-aged women sitting just behind them in the bed of the wagon.

"Good morning, folks," the lieutenant said, stepping up to the wagon. "My name's Lieutenant Ted Pitkin, and I'm in charge of this entrance. I'm glad to tell you that there are still plenty of 160-acre parcels of land available."

"We're not here to claim land, Lieutenant Pitkin," the man holding the reins said. "We're headed for Tahlequah to visit family."

Lieutenant Pitkin noticed the badge on the driver's vest. "I see you're sheriff of Dallas County, Texas."

"That's correct. I'm Sheriff Bradley Claiborne."

"Claiborne? Then I take it you're related to Chief of Police Britt Claiborne."

"He's my father."

"We think a lot of Chief Claiborne. And your mother is a lovely lady."

Bradley grinned. "You're right about that!" He then turned and introduced his wife, Wilma, his brother-in-law, Landry Lovegren, and Summer Dawn, his sister and Landry's wife.

"So you and Summer Dawn were raised here in the District?" the lieutenant said.

"That's right."

"Well, welcome home! You're free to just drive on to Tahlequah."

"Thank you, Lieutenant," Bradley said. "I'm surprised to hear you say that all the free land hasn't been claimed by now."

"We know prospective settlers are still coming from all

over the country. The government authorities in charge here figure it'll be several months yet before all the land has been claimed."

"I see. Well, Lieutenant Pitkin, it's been nice to meet you."

"You, too, Sheriff. I hope you folks have a nice visit with your family."

It was midmorning of the same day when Cherokee Rose finished sweeping and dusting the large cabin. She went to the kitchen and poured two glasses of cool buttermilk, then headed up the hall toward the front of the cabin. When she stepped onto the front porch, she saw that her father was dozing in his porch chair. At the sound of her footsteps, however, his head snapped up and he looked around.

"Thought I would rest out here a bit, Father." She extended the glass in her right hand toward him. "Would you like some buttermilk?"

"Of course," Walugo said, accepting the glass into his shaky hands. "Thank you." He took a long drink and smacked his lips. "Mm-mm! That really—as white people say—hits the spot!"

Cherokee Rose sat in the chair next to him and took a sip from her glass. They talked for a while about the covered wagons and men on horseback still moving past Tahlequah on their way to the land still available for claiming. They grew quiet for a few minutes, just sipping their buttermilk and watching butterflies flit around the porch. Then Cherokee Rose looked at Walugo and said, "I still marvel at your heroic deed last Monday evening."

The old man met her gaze and blinked. "What heroic deed was that, sweet girl?"

She chuckled. "Don't play ignorant with me. You know what I am talking about."

Walugo grinned at her shyly.

She reached over and took hold of his withered hand. "You are my hero. I am so proud of you."

Walugo caught sight of a covered wagon coming around the street corner, though he could not make out who the two men were on the driver's seat.

Cherokee Rose noticed that he was looking at something behind her and turned her head. She abruptly set her glass on a small table next to her and jumped to her feet, eyes wide. "Bradley! Landry!"

Walugo struggled to his feet and squinted at the face of the driver.

By the time Bradley Claiborne drew the wagon to a halt, Cherokee Rose and Walugo had stepped off the porch, and seconds later, both were being hugged by their guests.

When Cherokee Rose caught her breath, she wiped tears and said with a lilt in her voice, "Oh, I am so happy to see you! And Britt will be, too!" She flicked her tear-misted eyes from one face to the other. "Why did you not write to let us know you were coming?"

Bradley hugged his mother once more, then looked into her eyes. "Mama, we didn't write because we wanted to surprise you and Papa for your fiftieth wedding anniversary!"

Cherokee Rose shed more tears and hugged her son once again. She held him tight for a long moment, then she told each one how happy she was that they could be here for the celebration. She asked about her grandchildren and great-grandchildren and was told that everyone was fine and that they all sent their love and wished they could come, too.

"I was thinking maybe we should go to the police station right away and see Papa," Bradley said.

"Your father is probably not there," Cherokee Rose said. "He has been out of the office most of the time since the land rush started Monday, helping handle troublemakers. I am quite sure, however, that he will be home for lunch."

Bradley nodded. "I guess I'll just have to wait till then."

"If your father had known you were coming, no matter what the troublemakers were doing, he would have been right here to meet you! All right, Bradley, you and Landry bring everybody's bags inside. We may be a little crowded, but we will make room, even if I have to hang you boys from wall pegs!"

Bradley and Landry took four travel bags out of the wagon and headed toward the porch.

"You children must be tired," Cherokee Rose said with one arm around Summer Dawn's waist and the other around Wilma's. "You boys put the bags in the foyer, then come back out and sit here on the porch. You girls sit down here, too. I'll go to the kitchen and bring us out some coffee."

"Let us give you a hand, Mama," Summer Dawn said.

When Bradley and Landry moved from the foyer back out onto the porch, Walugo was settling himself with difficulty on the chair where he had been sitting.

Bradley knelt in front of his grandfather and noted the pain evident in his eyes. "Grandpa, you seem to be hurting. Are you all right?"

Walugo sighed a bit and nodded. "I am fine, Brad. Do not worry about me. Your mother does more than her share of that, believe me."

"I'm sure she does, Grandpa, but the rest of us care about you, too."

Walugo placed his hands on Bradley's shoulders. "Brad, my boy, I am ninety-one years old, so of course I have some aches and pains and a little shortness of breath at times. But I am very well cared for by your parents." He patted his grandson's shoulders and leaned back in his chair.

"Okay, if you say so." Bradley stood to his feet and gazed tenderly at his grandfather. "You think you're fooling me, Grandpa, but I can tell there's something more wrong than a few aches and pains. I know how you treasure your privacy, so I won't intrude any further."

Bradley turned and sat down on the porch step and leaned against the post. Summer Dawn and Wilma came out the door, each carrying a small tray with steaming cups of coffee, and Cherokee Rose was carrying a bowl of Bradley's favorite molasses cookies.

Bradley smiled at his mother and said, "I think somehow you knew I was coming, Mama, since you already had those cookies baked."

"You know I was not aware that you were coming. But sometimes I bake them just so I can feel close to you."

Bradley stood up and gave her another hug.

"And they happen to be your father's favorite cookies, too," she said with a twinkle in her eye.

The others laughed, even Walugo.

—∽—

It was almost noon when Craig and Gloria Parker emerged from the general store in Tahlequah, and Craig loaded groceries into their covered wagon.

"I can't wait to give the Beldens their new Bibles," he said to Gloria.

"I'm sure they won't be expecting them."

"That will make it just that much more enjoyable."

Craig helped Gloria onto the driver's seat and climbed up beside her. "Let's go by the Claiborne cabin and tell them about the Belden family receiving Jesus yesterday. Chief Claiborne's probably home now since it's just about lunchtime."

Craig picked up the reins and put the horses to a steady walk. Moments later, they drew up in front of the Claiborne cabin and noticed another wagon parked there and the police chief's horse tied to one of the hitching posts. Several people were talking and hugging in the front yard.

Cherokee Rose caught sight of the Parkers and beckoned them to join them. "Come and meet our son and daughter and their mates. They are here from Texas!"

Craig set the brake on the left front wheel and hopped down from the driver's seat. Gloria eased herself into Craig's arms as he reached up to her. When her feet touched ground, Craig took her hand, and they joined the happy family.

After introductions all around, Craig said, "Britt…Cherokee Rose, Gloria and I have some marvelous news for you."

Cherokee Rose smiled. "Let's hear it."

Craig and Gloria looked at each other.

"Go ahead, darling, you tell them!" Gloria said.

"Yesterday, we went over to the Beldens' place to let them know about the section of land we found and laid claim to," Craig said, his face beaming. "We had planned to talk to them about salvation while we were there, and the Lord blessed in a tremendous way. Gloria and I had the joy of leading all four of them to Jesus!"

Cherokee Rose clapped her hands together. "Oh, wonderful!"

"Yes!" said Britt, his eyes sparkling. "That is marvelous news!"

"They're coming to church Sunday to be baptized," Gloria said.

Britt then told the others about Craig and Gloria letting the Beldens have the choice piece of property with the creek running through it.

"I just know the Lord's going to bless them in a special way for this," Britt said.

"I think so, too," Cherokee Rose said. "Craig and Gloria, we have plenty of food. Would you do us the honor of eating lunch with us?"

Craig and Gloria exchanged glances, then Craig said, "We appreciate the invitation, Cherokee Rose, but we really should go and not infringe on this special time with your family."

"No! No!" Cherokee Rose said. "You will not be infringing. We want you to stay and eat with us. We would not think of sending you away hungry!"

Craig hunched his shoulders and looked at Gloria. "Well,

honey, we certainly wouldn't want to offend these nice people."

"Good!" Cherokee Rose said. "Follow me, everyone. Lunch is served."

After the meal, the Claibornes, the Lovegrens, and Walugo walked out of the house and followed the Parkers to their wagon. As Craig helped Gloria up onto the seat, she picked up the paper sack and said, "We bought some Bibles at the general store this morning to give to the Beldens. One for each of them. We're going to take them by their place on our way home."

"We're going to write down some Scripture passages for them to read, to help them grow spiritually," Craig said as he settled on the seat beside Gloria. "Well...it's been nice. See all of you on golden anniversary day at church!"

The Parker wagon passed from view, and Britt said, "Well, I must get back to the office. But before I go, Bradley, I want to congratulate you on the speed of your draw. When you got into the shoot-out with that infamous gunfighter Colby Slocum, you outdrew one of the fastest guns in the West. I'm mighty proud of you, son. And I'm mighty glad that you were the one who walked away."

"How did you get faster than a quick-draw gunfighter?" said Cherokee Rose, smiling at her son.

"Well, when I became a deputy sheriff, I figured that with a badge on my chest, I might just get challenged by gunfighters who love to brag about outdrawing and killing lawmen. So I started practicing...and I'm glad I did."

Britt grinned. "I'm glad you did, too."

Walugo nodded. "And so is your grandfather. It does not hurt to have the Lord on your side either."

"That's the most important part, Grandpa," Bradley said.

Britt looked around. "Well, folks, I must head for the office."

Summer Dawn stepped up to her parents and took hold of each one by the hand. "We're going to the general store to buy some groceries for Sunday dinner, because Wilma and I are going to cook up a real anniversary feast for the two of you."

"All right," Britt said, "but I'll give you the money to pay for the groceries."

Bradley shook his head. "No, Papa. We came prepared to buy all the groceries while we're here, and that includes the food for your anniversary dinner. No arguments. You can't spank me anymore, you know."

Britt chuckled. "I can still handle you, boy."

"If you give me any trouble, I'll have Grandpa Walugo take you down and sit on you!"

"You'd best not give that boy any trouble, Britt," Walugo said with a twinkle in his eye. "I would sure hate to embarrass you in front of this family by taking you down and sitting on you!"

"Since you're in such danger if you refuse to let us buy the groceries, Papa, am I going to hear words of surrender?" Bradley said.

Britt looked down into Cherokee Rose's eyes. She smiled, looked at her son, and said, "I will speak for your papa, Sheriff Bradley Claiborne. He humbly surrenders."

Everyone laughed, then Britt looked at Walugo. "I surrender only because I'm in such grave danger from you!"

The laughter grew louder.

seventeen

n Sunday morning, as people
filed into the church building
in Tahlequah, Pastor Joshudo
and Alanda were at the door to greet them.
The pastor and his wife had met Bradley and
Wilma and Landry and Summer Dawn
before, and they welcomed the two couples
warmly.

When Bradley and the pastor shook
hands, Bradley winced at Joshudo's grip.
"Whoa! I forgot what a powerful grip you
have, Pastor Joshudo."

Britt laid a hand on the pastor's shoulder
and said, "Son, maybe you don't remember

that for ten years running, before he went into the ministry, Pastor Joshudo was the Cherokee wrestling champion."

Bradley grinned and looked at his aching right hand. "Oh, yes, it all comes back to me now!"

Alanda smiled at her husband, then at Bradley. "I can still handle him when he disobeys me though."

Joshudo nodded vigorously. "That she can!"

The Claiborne family moved on into the auditorium, and the pastor and his wife welcomed the people who were next in line.

Inside, the Parkers and the Beldens were standing in the aisle talking. Britt and Cherokee Rose hurried up to them and told the Beldens how happy they were to learn that the Parkers had led them to the Lord.

Brent held up his brand-new Bible and said, "Look, Chief Claiborne! Look, Mrs. Claiborne! Mr. and Mrs. Parker gave us these Bibles!"

Britt nodded. "Very nice."

"These Parkers!" Kathy said. "I don't know what we're going to do with them. First, they let us have the land they had already picked out for themselves, then they came to our place and led us to Jesus…and now they gave us these beautiful Bibles!"

"I will tell you what to do with them," Cherokee Rose said. "Love them!"

"Oh, we do that, for sure!" Lee said. "How could we help but love them?"

Tears misted Kathy's eyes. "Thank God we'll be with them in heaven. And every day for all eternity, we'll remind them that we love them!"

⌒⌒

Outside, Martha Ackerman, her children, and her parents were headed to the church building when they saw Gene Vader standing on the porch, smiling at them. All three of Martha's children had taken a liking to their neighbor, who had come by to see them often.

They exchanged greetings, then Gene set his eyes on Martha and with a shy look said, "Ahhh, Martha…may I sit with you in the services today?"

Elizabeth took hold of her mother's hand and squeezed it. "Please, Mama. If you will let Mr. Vader sit next to you, I will sit on his other side."

Martha smiled at her children, then flashed the same smile at Gene Vader. "Of course, Gene. You're welcome to sit with me."

Elizabeth took hold of Gene's hand as they entered the church building, where they were greeted by Pastor Joshudo and Alanda. The children went to their Sunday school classrooms, and the adults went into the auditorium. When Sunday school was over, the Ackerman children came into the auditorium and sat with their mother, grandparents, and Gene Vader.

After the choir sang a rousing gospel song, Pastor Joshudo stepped up to the pulpit and made the usual announcements of upcoming events. Then he smiled and said, "I also have another announcement. A very important announcement. Chief Claiborne and Mrs. Claiborne…will you stand, please?"

When the Claibornes were on their feet, the pastor said, "Today is the fiftieth wedding anniversary for these precious people!"

The crowd applauded, then Pastor Joshudo told the story in brief how the two of them had met when Britt was an army lieutenant among the troops that conducted the North Carolina Cherokees westward to Indian Territory. He explained that they were both Christians when they met, then told how they fell in love and how the Lord made it possible for Britt to be honorably discharged from the army and become a police officer in Indian Territory.

With a broad smile on his face, Pastor Joshudo said, "They were married fifty years ago today…Sunday, April 28, 1839."

Again the people applauded.

The offering was then taken, and after a congregational hymn and a women's trio, Pastor Joshudo preached his sermon. At the close of the sermon, just before the invitation was given, Gene Vader leaned over to Martha and said, "I'm going to go forward and join the church."

"Wonderful!" Martha said. "My family and I are doing the same thing."

When the invitation was given, a few people walked the aisle to receive Jesus as their Saviour, the Beldens came forward to give their testimonies and present themselves for baptism, and Will and Essie Baker, Martha, Angie, and Eddie Ackerman, and Gene Vader came forward to join the church.

When the Beldens and those who had come for salvation had been baptized, there was much rejoicing all over the auditorium.

It was a warm, sunny spring day, and as the Claibornes and their son, daughter, and their mates, and Grandpa Walugo headed for the Claiborne cabin, the air was filled with the sweet fragrance of flowers and budding trees. When they arrived at the cabin, the men sat on the porch to await the call that dinner was ready.

Before Cherokee Rose reached the front door, Summer Dawn said, "Mama, Wilma and I will be taking care of cooking dinner today. It's your anniversary, so you are to stay here on the porch with Papa and these other men in your life."

Cherokee Rose shook her head. "Oh, but I could not do that. It is my responsibility to prepare dinner."

"Oh yes you *can* do that, Mama," Summer Dawn said. "You know you taught me quite well how to cook. And you've heard Bradley brag about what a wonderful cook Wilma is. So, please just sit down here by Papa and rest a while. Let us do the work."

Summer Dawn hugged her mother, then took her by the hand and led her to the rocking chair next to the straight-backed wooden chair where her father was sitting. Britt rose to his feet, smiling at his wife of fifty years.

As Cherokee Rose eased onto the rocker, Summer Dawn looked up at her father. "Papa, keep an eye on her, and don't let her get up till Wilma and I call all of you to dinner."

Britt chuckled and winked at his daughter. "I'll do my best, honey, but you know your mother has a mind of her own." He bent down and kissed his wife's cheek.

Cherokee Rose looked up at her daughter. "All right, Summer Dawn. I will be good."

"Promise?"

"I promise."

As Summer Dawn and Wilma entered the cabin,

Cherokee Rose looked at her husband with a twinkle in her eye. "You know, darling, it really is good to be waited on for a change. Guess I will just sit here and enjoy it."

An hour and a half later, when the family was at the dinner table, there was much laughter, and many precious memories were shared as they all enjoyed the delicious dinner of roast chicken, mashed potatoes smothered in gravy, tasty vegetables, and hot rolls, as well as cool tea.

Summer Dawn and Wilma had baked a three-tiered white cake and a custard pie, but when they carried them from the cupboard to the table, everyone agreed that they were too full. They would wait and eat their dessert after the evening church service.

It was a grand and happy day and one that Britt and Cherokee Rose would put in the memory books of their minds and bring out to enjoy often together in the years to come.

The next morning, Cherokee Rose was awake and up earlier than usual. Britt was still asleep as she dressed and made her way to the kitchen.

A sad feeling filled her heart as she cooked a large breakfast for her family. Standing over the stove, she said, "Lord, I know Britt and I are exactly where You want us, and I know our children are, too. But You understand this mother's heart. You know how much I miss them and long to be near them. Help me to always remember Your Word through the apostle Paul,

'I have learned, in whatsoever state I am, therewith to be content.' Help me, dear Lord, to be grateful that we have had these few days to enjoy together, and please keep them safe as they return to their homes in Texas."

Cherokee Rose moved to the kitchen window and looked out at God's beautiful handiwork. She was unaware that Britt had quietly paused at the kitchen door a few minutes earlier and had heard a portion of her prayer.

He moved across the kitchen, stepped up behind her, and touched her shoulder. As she turned to him, he said, "Having some difficulty with the children heading home today?"

The tears she had been holding back welled up in her eyes and began to trickle down her cheeks. She nodded and said with quivering lips, "Yes, darling. It—it is so hard to let them go."

Britt took her into his arms. "I know. It's hard for me, too. I love you so much, my precious one." She laid her head on his chest as she shed the tears that seemed to be coming all the way from her heart.

After a few moments, Cherokee Rose eased back from her husband's arms and dried her tears with her apron. She went to her tiptoes, planted a kiss on Britt's lips, then looked into his eyes. "I love you, Britt Claiborne. You always know just what I need. Thank you."

"I guess after fifty years I should know you pretty well. I knew this morning would be hard for you."

They heard footsteps coming down the hall, and Bradley and Wilma and Summer Dawn and Landry entered the kitchen, the delectable aroma of breakfast drawing them. Soon Walugo shuffled his way into the kitchen too.

—⁊

After breakfast, Summer Dawn and Wilma helped Cherokee Rose clean up the kitchen, then they all made their way outside to the covered wagon. Many tears were shed as good-byes were said, and Bradley, Wilma, Landry, and Summer Dawn drove away, heading back to Texas.

eighteen

y the end of April, five new towns had been established in Oklahoma District: Guthrie, Edmond, Oklahoma City, Moore, and Norman.

Guthrie already had over ten thousand people living in covered wagons and tents. The other towns each had over five thousand who were doing the same, and plans were underway to begin building houses. These people had come from many parts of the United States and Territories, not desiring to be farmers but wanting to make their homes in Oklahoma District, which government experts had predicted would become a desirable place to live.

The railroad companies were laying tracks across the District at amazing speed, keeping work crews alternating day and night. Water towers and other requirements for steam rail operation were rapidly being built at intervals along the tracks.

Construction crews from Missouri, Arkansas, and Texas were quickly erecting business buildings in all five of the new towns. Medical doctors were having clinics built, merchants were preparing to open stores, and each town was getting a bank.

In order to strengthen their finances, men who owned land and were planting crops also worked on the construction crews.

Spring rains were coming two or three times a week, which made the farmers happy.

By the end of April, the soldiers who had come from neighboring states had left the District to return to their forts. The Fort Gibson soldiers and the federal deputy marshals, however, were having to deal with frequent confrontations between white men and Indians. United Cherokee Nation Police Chief Britt Claiborne and his officers were also forced to deal with these problems.

On Wednesday, May 1, Chief United States Marshal Robert Landon called for a meeting of his deputies, as well as Police Chief Britt Claiborne and Fort Gibson's commandant, General Lloyd Caldwell, at the fort's assembly hall.

Landon had Chief Claiborne and General Caldwell come

to the platform and stand beside him before he started the meeting. Once the deputy marshals were all seated, Landon opened the meeting by bringing up the problems they were having with the Indians giving the white settlers trouble.

"I'm glad, men, that so far no one on either side has been seriously injured or killed," Landon said. "I can sympathize with the Indians because for over half a century our government has broken promise after promise to them. But this is no fault of the white settlers who have come here by invitation of the government to fulfill their dreams of living in this fertile land. I hope the Indians learn to live with things as they are pretty soon. Otherwise I fear the situation will only get worse."

"My men are doing all they can to keep that from happening," Britt said.

"And so are mine," Caldwell said.

Britt rubbed the back of his neck. "Of course, sometimes the altercations have been started by white men who simply do not like Indians."

Marshal Landon sighed and looked out at his deputies. "You men will have to watch out for this, too. I certainly hope that peace will come between the whites and the Indians before someone is seriously injured or killed."

There were a few seconds of silence, then Marshal Landon said, "I have one other thing to bring up. I have been in contact by telegraph with President Benjamin Harrison on the subject of the sooners. As you all know, they are still being held in the Oklahoma District Prison at Tahlequah. The president agrees with me that since the land rush is over and there is still plenty of farmland available, the sooners who showed no resistance when they were arrested should now be released and allowed to claim property. Does anyone here disagree?"

When no one objected, Landon smiled and said, "Good! President Harrison will be glad to hear that we are in agreement. Well, men, that's all. Meeting dismissed."

Marshal Landon turned to Caldwell and Claiborne and said, "I'd like for you two to go with me to the prison to tell the sooners the good news."

A half hour later, Warden Yukindo and two guards gathered the sooners in the prison into a large room and told them to sit on the floor. When they were all settled, Yukindo said to the guard who stood by the door, "All right, Clibino, bring our guests in."

All eyes were fixed on the door as Chief U.S. Marshal Robert Landon, General Lloyd Caldwell, and Police Chief Britt Claiborne stepped into the room. Britt locked eyes with Clete Hobbs, who was seated near the front, and smiled at him. Hobbs blinked and managed to give him a thin grin.

The men listened intently as Landon told them of his telegraph correspondence with President Benjamin Harrison and that he and the president agreed that since these men had not resisted the authorities when they were arrested, they were going to be released from the prison.

There was instant joy on the men's faces, and it grew even brighter when he told them that not only would they be released, but they were each welcome to choose 160 acres of land and bring their families into the District.

Clete Hobbs raised his hand and asked Marshal Landon if he could speak. Landon granted him permission, and Hobbs stood to his feet, wiped tears, and looked at Britt, saying, "Chief Claiborne, I want you to know that I am so ashamed of myself for having snuck into the District illegally. I was so wrong in what I did to your friend Craig Parker. Please forgive me, Chief Claiborne."

Britt smiled. "You are forgiven, Mr. Hobbs."

Suddenly, more men stood and began to admit their wrongdoing. One after another, they thanked Landon, Claiborne, and Caldwell for setting them free.

On Friday afternoon, May 3, a forty-two-year-old settler named Nate Hatton was plowing a field on his 160 acres a few miles south of Tahlequah. His sixteen-year-old son, Barry, walked beside him as Nate guided the horse that was pulling the plow.

Nate caught movement on the nearby road that ran along the east side of his property, and he looked up to see a small band of Cherokee men riding their horses slowly along the road.

Barry saw the Indians, too, and noticed his father glaring at them. When the Cherokees passed from view, Nate spit on the ground, his hate-filled eyes fixed on the last place he saw them.

"Papa, are you going to carry that hatred for Indians inside you for the rest of your life?" Barry asked.

Nate swung his hot gaze to his son. "I've told you plenty of times, they killed my brother at the Little Big Horn battle. And I will *die* hating them!"

"But Papa, the Indians who killed Uncle Nick were not

Cherokees, they were Sioux. And besides, that was almost thirteen years ago. Like Mama has told you a thousand times, your
hatred is going to dry you up inside."

Nate spit on the ground again. "It doesn't matter which
tribe killed my brother. An Indian is an Indian, and I'm never
gonna stop hating them! If I had my way, Barry, they'd all be
wiped off the face of the earth!"

The sixteen-year-old boy shook his head. "Papa, I'm going
to our wagon to chop wood for Mama. She needs it to cook
supper."

Nate nodded, gripping the plow handles and calling for
the horse to move faster. He kept an eye on Barry as he headed
toward the Hatton wagon, which could not be seen from the
field where he was plowing.

A few minutes after Barry had passed from view, Nate saw
a small tree directly in front of him. He had already chopped
down two other small trees that day and placed them in the
nearby cart. He pressed back against the reins, and the horse
came to a halt, blowing hard through its nostrils. Nate hurried
to the cart and reached inside for his hatchet.

He looked up to see a pinto stallion trotting across his
field, having come from the nearby road. Nate laid his hatchet
down, picked up some dirt clods, and threw them at the pinto,
shouting angrily, "Get off my property!"

Frightened by the dirt clods, the pinto galloped away and
soon was out of sight.

Nate picked up the hatchet and went to the small tree,
chopped it down, then carried it to the cart and placed it with
the two trees he had cut down earlier. At the same moment, he
saw a young Cherokee man walking toward him from the road.

As the Cherokee, who appeared to be about twenty years of age, drew up, he asked in perfect English, "Sir, have you seen a pinto stallion anywhere in this area?"

"No, I have not! How dare you come on this property! Don't you know it is forbidden by District law for an Indian to trespass on a white man's property?"

The young Indian spoke softly, "I am sorry, sir, but I am only trying to find my horse. I was sure a decent white man would not mind."

Nate gripped the hatchet handle till his knuckles turned white. "So I'm not a decent white man, eh?" he hissed through his teeth.

With a shriek of rage, Nate struck the Cherokee on the side of his head with the blade of the hatchet, and he went down. Breathing heavily through his nostrils, Nate jerked the hatchet blade out of the deep wound it had made, then bent over the Indian and cupped his hand over the Indian's nose and mouth, which was sagging open. There was no breath.

Standing up straight, Nate did a quick panorama and was glad to see there was no one in sight. He went to the cart and tossed in the hatchet, then took out a shovel. He dragged the young Cherokee's body onto a plowed area on the other side of a grassy knoll, where no one could see him from the road, and started digging.

While he was digging hard and fast, Nate Hatton felt elation that he was actually burying an Indian.

At sundown, in a Cherokee village on the edge of a reservation only three miles west of Nate Hatton's land, a Cherokee woman in her early forties was cooking supper in the kitchen of the cabin.

The back door of the cabin came open, and the woman looked at the young man who entered the kitchen. She smiled and said, "Rustino, did you find your pinto?"

The young man grinned. "Mother, Rustino has not come back yet."

"Oh, I am so sorry, Justino. You know how I have a hard time telling my twin sons apart since my eyesight has gotten worse."

"Mother, you had that problem even when Rustino and I were little boys, and so did Father, bless his memory."

The mother smiled weakly. "You need to wash your hands. Supper is almost ready. We will have to go ahead and eat, even though your brother is not back yet."

Supper was ready by the time Justino had washed and dried his hands. The mother and son sat down at the kitchen table to eat, hoping that Rustino would soon return.

When it was bedtime, the missing twin still had not returned. Justino tried to comfort his mother by saying that his brother loved the horse so much that he would probably not come home until he found him.

The next morning at breakfast, Justino looked across the table at his mother, whose eyes were swollen from crying a good part of the night, and said, "Mother, I am going to go look for Rustino as soon as I am through with breakfast."

She wiped tears from her eyes. "Justino, some white men can be very cruel to us Indians." She touched her chest. "I have this terrible ache inside. I fear for your brother. What if a white settler has caught him on his land, chasing that pinto of his?"

Justino reached across the table and patted her hand. "Do not worry, Mother. I will find him."

She tried to smile. It was a faint one, but she nodded and said, "You are a good boy, Justino."

After breakfast, Justino went to the small corral and barn behind the cabin, bridled and saddled his horse, and led the animal to the front of the house, where his mother was waiting. He embraced her, spoke some more words of encouragement, then mounted and put the horse to a gallop.

The mother watched her son ride away, then closed her eyes, seized by an icy, uncontrollable fear.

Late that afternoon, Justino was riding his bay stallion toward home. He had not found his twin brother, nor his pinto. Suddenly, he caught sight of a white farmer plowing his field close by the road, and he decided to ask him if he had seen the pinto or his brother.

Nate Hatton was bent over the plow, unhitching it from his horse, when he heard footsteps on the soft earth behind him. He straightened up, thinking it was Barry, and turned around.

When he saw the face of the Cherokee man approaching him, his heart froze. Terror closed over him like a powerful fist. A stab of pain lanced his heart, and he shook with horror, gasped, and collapsed.

Justino dashed to the white man and knelt beside him. He placed an ear over the man's sagging mouth to see if he was breathing. He was not. Justino quickly checked for a pulse. There was none.

Justino's throat went dry. With his heart pounding, he turned around and scanned the road. There was no one in sight. He ran back to the road, mounted his horse, and put the stallion to a gallop.

nineteen

The next day, Sunday, May 5, Pastor Joshudo and Alanda were at the front door of the church building as usual, greeting the members and visitors coming for the morning services.

Gene Vader was with Martha Ackerman, her children, and Will and Essie Baker as the pastor and his wife greeted them. They moved on inside the auditorium and soon were talking with Craig and Gloria Parker. After a few minutes, Gene and Martha and her children moved down the aisle toward their favorite pew.

"I really like Gene Vader," Craig said to Will and Essie. "He seems like a nice fellow."

"Oh, he is," Will said.

"We noticed last Sunday that he sat with all of you," Gloria said.

"And that he sat next to Martha," added Craig with a wry grin.

"It's quite obvious that Martha and Gene are attracted to each other," Will said. "I guess you both know about his wife and children getting killed a few years ago."

"Yes, we heard that," Gloria said. "And with both of their mates gone, I'm sure Martha and Gene are finding solace in each other."

"I'll share a little secret with you," Will said. "Essie and I like Gene very much. He's a dedicated Christian, and he has been a help to me, too. He comes by our place regularly, and on several occasions he's helped me with some project. We're praying that one day the Lord will bring Gene and Martha together as husband and wife. Martha's children really love Gene…especially little Elizabeth."

Essie smiled. "Our daughter needs a husband, and our grandchildren need a father. In our minds, Gene is perfect for their needs."

Craig nodded. "And Gene, having lost his children as well as his wife, will find his needs fulfilled, too, I'd say."

The Parkers headed toward a section of pews on the right side of the auditorium, and the Bakers moved down the center aisle. Will and Essie found Martha, Gene, and the children still standing in the aisle, talking to another family. When the family saw the Bakers drawing up, they greeted them, then excused themselves.

"Well, let's sit down," Will said.

Gene looked at Martha questioningly and smiled.

She smiled back. "I think you and I sort of have an unspoken agreement, Gene."

As the family filed into the chosen row, Elizabeth slipped past her mother, reached up, and took hold of Gene's hand. Gene looked down at the pretty little girl and smiled. Elizabeth tugged on his hand, and Gene leaned down close to her.

"Can I sit beside you again?" she whispered.

"Of course, sweetie, if it's all right with your mother."

"Oh, she won't mind." The little four-year-old grinned happily and climbed up onto the pew.

"Seems that you and Elizabeth have an unspoken agreement, too," Martha said.

Gene slipped his arm around Elizabeth. "Isn't it great!"

After the morning service, Essie tapped Gene on the arm and said, "We would like for you to come to our place for Sunday dinner."

"Thank you. I would be most happy to, Mrs. Baker," Gene said.

"Oh, goody!" Elizabeth said.

"We always love it when you come to our place," Angie said. "It will be so much fun to have you eat with us this time."

"I'm in full accord with Essie and my grandchildren, Gene." Will looked at his daughter. "How about you, Martha?"

Martha put on a false frown. "Oh, I suppose I can stand having him at our table."

Everybody laughed, including Gene Vader.

They all headed for their wagons and came upon Britt and Cherokee Rose Claiborne and Walugo. As they walked along together, moving slowly for Walugo's sake, Walugo moved up beside Gene Vader and said in a low voice, "My heart goes out to you, son. I know what it is like to have your wife die."

Gene nodded and smiled at him. "It isn't easy, even for a Christian man, is it Walugo?"

"No, sir. It will not be long, though, till I join my precious Naya in heaven."

Britt took hold of Cherokee Rose's hand and gave her a compassionate look.

Walugo noticed and moved a couple of steps closer to her, and with a shade of regret in his voice, said, "Daughter, I am sorry. I did not know you could hear me."

Cherokee Rose looked at him through a mist of tears. "It is all right, Father. I understand that you miss Mother so very much."

At the Baker place, a large table was placed beside their covered wagon. When dinner was on the table and Essie told everyone to sit down, little Elizabeth maneuvered herself up close to Gene Vader. She grinned up at him as she wiggled up onto the chair next to the one he had chosen, as if to say, "Here I am, just like we planned."

Gene pulled out the chair on the other side of him for Martha, then eased onto his chair. He put his arm around Elizabeth and hugged her up close to his side. He looked at Martha, and she smiled sweetly at him, a thin film of tears shining in her eyes.

Will called on Gene to lead them in prayer, and when he finished, the food was started around the table. Dinner was a lively time, with much chatter and laughter punctuating the warm afternoon air.

When the meal was over, Gene turned to Martha. "Would you do me a favor?"

"What's that?" she asked, smiling.

"Would you take a walk with me into those woods over there on your parents' property?"

Martha started to say something, but Essie jumped in ahead. "I think it would be nice for the two of you to go for a walk."

"You go on and take that walk, Martha," Will said. "I'll help your mother with the dishes."

"I'll help, too," Angie said.

"Me, too," put in Eddie.

Elizabeth looked at her mother. "I don't want to help clean up this time, Mama. I want to go for a walk with you and Mr. Vader."

Essie set her gaze on Elizabeth. "Oh, no you don't, little girl. I really need your help here, and besides, I know a little girl who needs to take a nap so she'll be awake for church this evening."

Elizabeth turned and looked at her mother, than back at her grandmother. "All right, Grandma. If you say so."

Gene and Martha strolled slowly across the open fields, talking about their new life in Oklahoma District and about their mates who had passed on. Both of them admitted that they had lonely spots in their hearts. When they entered the shade of the trees, they found two aging tree stumps side by side, and after taking Martha's hand and seating her on one of the stumps, Gene sat down on the other one, facing her.

After sitting and talking for about half an hour, Gene suggested they get back to her family.

They had been gone for just over an hour when they drew up to the Baker wagon and found Elizabeth asleep in her grandmother's arms.

"Well, Mama, you were right about that little girl who needed to take a nap," Martha said.

"Mm-hmm. She's so much like her mother was at this age."

The Bakers looked on with pleasure as their other two grandchildren dashed to Gene, the warm feelings evident between them.

That evening at the church in Tahlequah, Cherokee Rose was sitting between Britt and her father, and they both noticed that Walugo's breathing became labored during one of the congregational hymns.

Cherokee Rose leaned close to her father and spoke just loud enough for him to hear her above the singing, "Father, are you all right?"

Britt was looking past Cherokee Rose at Walugo as the old man touched a hand to his chest and said in a voice that was thin and reedy, "I am just a little tired. I will be all right after I get a good night's rest."

Britt looked at his wife. "Honey, let's take him home."

Walugo gave his son-in-law a weak smile. "That is not necessary, Britt. I can make it through the rest of the service. I want to hear the pastor's sermon."

When the service was over and the Claibornes headed for home in their wagon, Walugo sat on the driver's seat between his daughter and son-in-law, with Cherokee Rose holding his hand.

"I think we should take you to one of the doctors at the clinic," Britt said.

Walugo shook his head. "It is not necessary. I will feel better after I get a good night's rest."

"Father, I wish you would let us take you to one of the doctors," Cherokee Rose said.

The old man patted her hand. "My child, I am nearly ninety-two years old. God has cared for me all these years. I do not want some doctor poking around on me. I am so very tired. If it is God's time for me to go to my final home, no doctor can change that anyway."

Cherokee Rose felt tears moisten her eyes. "Oh, Father, I guess I have been selfish wanting to keep you here with me. I know how tired you are, and I know you are having a lot of pain these days. I...I won't be selfish anymore. I will just pray for the Lord's will to be done."

Britt watched as Walugo lifted his gnarled hands and cupped his daughter's face in them. "Thank you for understanding. The time has to be getting close for me to go to heaven and see my Saviour and be reunited with my beloved Naya."

The tears were now streaming down Cherokee Rose's cheeks. "I love you, Father," she said, looking into his eyes by the light of the streetlamps.

Walugo kissed her cheek. "I love you, too, my sweet Cherokee Rose."

Britt sent a silent prayer heavenward, asking for God's grace and mercy on the dear old man and the daughter who loved him so much.

Late that night, lying side by side with moonlight streaming through their bedroom window, Britt and Cherokee Rose talked about Walugo's declining health, and she wiped tears from her eyes with the bedsheet as she said, "I know Father wants to go home to heaven so he can be with his Saviour and with Mother. I…I can't blame him. But it's so hard."

"I know, sweetheart," said Britt, taking hold of her hand. "Let's pray."

In his prayer, Britt asked that the Lord's will be done, and he also asked that whenever the day came that it was His time to take Walugo home, He would give Cherokee Rose the peace and comfort she would need.

On Monday morning at the Claiborne cabin, Cherokee Rose was preparing breakfast at the cookstove when Britt came into the kitchen, having just shaved. She turned and said, "Sweetheart, I looked in on Father while you were shaving, and he was still asleep. Will you go and see if he is awake, please? Breakfast will be ready in a few minutes."

"Of course." Britt entered the hall and made his way through the cabin to his father-in-law's room. He tapped on the door, and when there was no response, he opened the door and stepped in.

The elderly Walugo was awake, but still in bed. He was

gasping for breath while clutching his chest. He looked up at Britt and said hoarsely, "It is my heart. I know it is…my time, Britt. I want to go and be with Jesus…and with my precious Naya."

"I'll go get one of the doctors at the clinic."

Walugo rolled his head on the pillow. "No, son. It will do no good. Thank you for caring for me…all these years. You…have always been so special to me. I am ready to go to my real Land of Promise. God bless you, Britt."

The dying man choked slightly and raised a trembling hand toward Britt. As Britt took hold of it, Walugo said, "Please tell my…dear daughter that I love her and that…she has been the joy of my life."

Walugo coughed again, smiled, and took his last breath. As he let it out, his eyes closed, and his body went limp.

Britt heard footsteps behind him as he was feeling for a pulse in the old man's neck. He left the bedside, and when Cherokee Rose looked at him questioningly, he nodded, then opened his arms to her and embraced her. She clung to him and broke into sobs. When her sobbing began to ease, he told her the last words her father had said.

On Wednesday morning, May 8, 1889, Pastor Joshudo conducted the graveside service in the cemetery just outside Tahlequah. A large crowd of Indians and whites had assembled. In his message, the pastor quoted Walugo's final words. Many tears were shed, but hearts were blessed by Walugo's words about going to his real Land of Promise.

Tears flowed unchecked down Cherokee Rose's cheeks as

she stood beside her father's coffin. Britt was beside her, with his arm around her. She put out her hand, gently caressed the closed lid, and whispered, "You were the most wonderful father a girl could ever have. You have taught me so much and have given to me so abundantly. Rest in peace in our blessed Saviour's arms, Father. I love you."

And in the gentle breeze that rustled the leaves of the nearby trees, she could almost hear her father reply, "I love you, too, my sweet Cherokee Rose."

twenty

n Thursday, May 9, Pastor Joshudo walked into the front office of Oklahoma District's only newspaper, the *Cherokee Phoenix*, headquartered in Tahlequah. Behind the counter was a young Cherokee man with whom the pastor was acquainted.

"Hello, Pastor Joshudo."

"Hello, Newtino. I would like to see reporter Vokini, if he is here."

"Yes, he is here. I will fetch him for you. Did you like the article he wrote in today's edition?"

"Very much so," Joshudo said. "I just wanted to express my appreciation to him. I was amazed to see it on the front page."

The pastor let his gaze roam over the office while he waited for the reporter, and in a few minutes, Newtino came through the door with Vokini on his heels.

"Hello, Pastor Joshudo," Vokini said as he stepped up to the counter. "Newtino told me you liked the article on today's front page."

Joshudo reached across the counter, and they shook hands. "I saw you at the funeral, but I did not realize you were there to write an article about it."

"Our editor asked me to, Pastor, because Walugo was the father-in-law of Chief of Police Britt Claiborne. He thought it would be interesting reading for everyone in the District."

"Well, you did a wonderful job on it, Vokini. And I very much appreciate your quoting Walugo's last words."

"Well, Pastor, those were inspiring words about going to the real Land of Promise."

"Heaven is that, all right, for those who know the Lord Jesus Christ as their Saviour," Joshudo said. "You have visited our services a couple of times. What about when *you* die, Vokini? Will you go to the real Land of Promise?"

Vokini's features pinched slightly. "Well, Pastor, from what you showed from the Bible, I do not believe so. I would like to know more about it though."

Joshudo smiled. "I have time to talk right now if you would like."

The reporter's face flushed. "I would like to talk about it, but I cannot right now, Pastor. I am about to leave to do some interviews for tomorrow's edition."

Joshudo smiled again. "Well, how about coming to church next Sunday morning? Listen to another sermon; then if it clears up your questions, walk the aisle at the invitation as you have seen others do, and you can settle it. If not, we will talk after the service, and I will help you."

Vokini glanced toward his friend. "Newtino, would you like to go to Pastor Joshudo's church with me next Sunday?"

"Why, yes, I would," Newtino said.

"Good, my friends," the pastor said. "I will look for you on Sunday. And Vokini...thank you again for that article."

On Friday, Cherokee Rose was shopping for groceries at Tahlequah's general store. A small group of women, both white and Indian, gathered around her to express their condolences about her father's death.

In the store at the same time was Corrie Gerson, who had read the article in the *Cherokee Phoenix* the day before. Pausing in the aisle of shelves unnoticed, Corrie listened to Cherokee Rose as she told the women about her father's faith in the Lord Jesus Christ. Her voice quavering, Cherokee Rose said, "I can gladly tell you that Father is now in the real Land of Promise...heaven."

Corrie's desire to know more about Jesus Christ once again arose strongly in her heart. Even though her atheist husband did not want his wife nor their fourteen-year-old daughter to have anything to do with what he called the "Jesus crowd," Corrie's desire to learn of Jesus was stronger then her fear of Gilbert's anger.

When the group of women walked away, leaving Cherokee

Rose dabbing at her eyes with a handkerchief, Corrie came up to her and said in a soft tone, "Mrs. Claiborne, my name is Corrie Gerson. My husband, teenage daughter, and I are from Kansas."

Cherokee Rose sniffed, dabbed at her eyes once more, and smiled. "You are settlers here?"

"Yes, ma'am. I read the article in yesterday's paper about your father's funeral, and a little while ago I overheard those ladies talking to you. Please accept my sympathy for the loss of your father."

"Thank you," Cherokee Rose said. "I am glad to meet you, Mrs. Gerson."

"Ma'am, I…ah…was quite touched when I read your father's last words before he died, saying he was going to the real Land of Promise. And I heard you telling those other women of your father's faith in Jesus Christ." Corrie cleared her throat gently. "Mrs. Claiborne, sometime soon may I meet with you so you can tell me about Jesus and about heaven and hell? I know so very little about the Christian faith."

Cherokee Rose's heart quickened pace. "I will be heading for home as soon as I finish shopping. Could you come home with me now?"

"We live some six miles southwest of Tahlequah," Corrie said, her eyes sparkling, "and my husband won't be coming to pick me up here for at least another three hours. He has a lot of work to do."

"Our cabin is only a few minutes' walk from here," Cherokee Rose said. "Let's get the rest of our groceries. I'm sure the clerk will allow you to leave your groceries here if you explain the situation to him."

—☙—

When Cherokee Rose and Corrie arrived at the Claiborne cabin, Cherokee Rose put her groceries away. Then they went to the parlor, where she picked up her Bible from a small table beside the sofa, and they sat down together.

Cherokee Rose asked Corrie what she knew about the Christian faith, and Corrie explained that she had been raised in a home where there was no Bible and the family never attended church. She married Gilbert Gerson, who also was raised in a home like hers.

Corrie had picked up from things she had heard and read over the years that Jesus had no human father; that by the miracle of the virgin birth He came into this world as the Son of God to provide for sinners the way of salvation from a burning place called hell. She knew that Jesus had been crucified and that three days later He arose from the grave and soon went back to heaven…and that somehow, if guilty sinners put their faith in Him, they would go to heaven when they died.

Cherokee Rose looked her square in the eye. "Corrie, do you believe all those things that you just told me are true?"

"Yes, I do. I don't understand them all, but I do believe them. I just don't understand how Jesus' death, burial, and resurrection provide salvation for sinners, nor exactly what a sinner like me has to do to be forgiven and be saved."

"Well, the answers to your questions are right here in God's Word. Let me show you. You can read every passage with me."

Eagerness showed in Corrie Gerson's eyes.

With a prayer in her heart, Cherokee Rose opened her Bible and took Corrie from Scripture to Scripture. Corrie often had questions, and Cherokee Rose answered them patiently. With tears in her eyes, and with her new friend leading her, Corrie called on Jesus Christ and received Him into her heart as her Saviour.

Cherokee Rose hugged Corrie, then showed her in the Bible that her next act of obedience to God as a Christian was to come to church and be baptized.

Tears misted Corrie's eyes, and her lips trembled as she said, "Mrs. Claiborne, I won't be able to do that. I certainly want to obey God and be baptized…but there's something I haven't told you."

Cherokee Rose's brow furrowed. "What is that?"

"Well, you see…Gilbert is an adamant atheist. He has never wanted me or our daughter to have anything to do with churches of any kind, but especially those that preach Jesus Christ. He calls them the 'Jesus crowd.' He won't let me come to church."

Cherokee Rose hugged Corrie again. "With prayer, all things are possible. I will tell my husband about you receiving Jesus as your Saviour today, and we will be praying that Gilbert will not only let you be baptized, but that he will let you come to church regularly. We will also pray that the Lord will bring him and your daughter to Jesus, too."

Tears were streaming down Corrie's cheeks. "Oh, thank you. I can pray that way, too, can't I?"

"Yes! You are now a child of God, and He wants you to come to Him with your burdens and problems. He is a great big wonderful God, Corrie. With our prayers, He can bring about whatever He deems necessary to bring Gilbert out of his atheism and to Himself."

Corrie palmed tears from her cheeks. "Yes! Oh, yes! I will pray hard!"

Cherokee Rose stood to her feet. "In order to grow in your faith, you must read and study God's Word every day." She went to a nearby desk and took a brand-new Bible out of a drawer and handed it to Corrie. "I bought this Bible to send to one of my great-granddaughters in Texas, but I will buy her another one."

"Mrs. Claiborne, you are so kind and so generous. Thank you. I will treasure this Bible, especially since you gave it to me. And…thank you for leading me to Jesus. I already have such peace in my heart."

Cherokee Rose's eyes misted. "I am so glad, Corrie. Only the Prince of Peace can put that in your heart."

Corrie threw her arms around Cherokee Rose, and the two women held on to each other for a long moment, then eased back in one another's arms.

"And since we are now sisters in Christ, please call me Cherokee Rose."

Corrie wiped tears from her eyes and said, "All right, Mrs. Claiborne…I mean, Cherokee Rose."

Gilbert Gerson swung his covered wagon to a halt in front of the general store in Tahlequah. Corrie was there waiting, her large purse in hand and the groceries in bags at her feet. Gilbert helped her up onto the seat beside Peggy, quickly loaded the groceries into the rear of the wagon, and climbed up to the driver's seat and put the horses in motion.

As the wagon rolled along the street, Peggy noticed her

mother's hands were shaking. "Mama, are you all right?"

"Of course, honey. Why do you ask?"

"You seem a bit nervous."

"Yes, you do," Gilbert said. "I noticed your hand was trembling when I helped you up on the seat. What's wrong?"

With a prayer in her heart for help from the Lord, Corrie looked at her husband and said, "I have something to tell you."

She then told her husband about reading in the newspaper about Police Chief Britt Claiborne's father-in-law's death and about meeting Cherokee Rose Claiborne at the general store. She told Gilbert that she had gone to the Claiborne home where Mrs. Claiborne showed her from the Bible how to become a Christian. She then took the Bible from her purse and showed it to Gilbert, explaining that Mrs. Claiborne had given it to her after she had received Jesus Christ into her heart as her Saviour.

Gilbert's eyes flashed fire. "I don't want that Bible in our house! I'm gonna burn it when we get home!"

Tears welled up in Corrie's eyes, blurring her vision as she turned toward Gilbert. "No, Gilbert, please don't do this to me! If you love me, please don't take my Bible from me."

Peggy touched her father's arm. "Please, Papa. I want Mama to be happy."

Gilbert Gerson licked his lips, looked past Peggy at Corrie, and said, "All right, all right. You can keep your Bible, but one thing I'm telling you right now—don't try to push this salvation stuff on Peggy or me. You hear me?"

Corrie looked at him, his words hanging between them like an impending storm.

"You hear me!" he bellowed.

Corrie glanced at her daughter, who had a hopeless look in her eyes, then set her gaze on Gilbert. "I hear you."

When the Gersons arrived at their property, Gilbert parked the wagon in its usual spot, hopped to the ground, and helped his wife and daughter down from the seat. He then unhitched the horses and headed back to one of his fields, leaving Corrie and Peggy to arrange the groceries in the small cupboard of the wagon.

When they were finished, they climbed down out of the wagon. Peggy looked at her mother with pleading eyes and said, "Mama…"

"Yes, honey?"

"I…I know Papa doesn't want you to tell me about Jesus, but please…show me from your Bible how to be saved. I want to go to heaven, too."

Corrie glanced in the direction her husband had gone some twenty minutes earlier, then turned to her daughter and said, "When we have the time alone, I promise I will show you all about it. I want you to be saved, too. But…your father could come back any minute and interrupt us." She looked back over her shoulder, fearful that he might already be on his way to the wagon.

"Okay, Mama, I understand. I'll wait until you and I have some time alone. But I hope it's soon."

Corrie patted her cheek. "It will be, honey. The Lord will see to that. And when you do get saved, the Lord is going to work in your papa's mind so he won't give us trouble about our faith."

Corrie took the water bucket from the side of the covered wagon. "Honey, would you go to the well and fill the bucket for me, please? I need to do some scrubbing in the wagon."

"Sure," said Peggy, taking the bucket from her mother. "I'll be right back."

The well was some distance from the wagon. As Peggy walked that direction among tall green plants, suddenly she heard a rattling sound, accompanied by a sharp hiss. She stopped, and less than three feet from her she saw a coiled rattlesnake, it's black eyes glistening, its tongue flitting in and out.

The sight of the snake went through Peggy like an electric shock. She wheeled to dash away, but the rattler struck. Its fangs punctured the calf of her left leg, and Peggy stumbled and fell. Pain like the sting of a thousand wasps exploded in her leg and shot up to her hip.

Lying on the ground, her heart pounding, Peggy gritted her teeth and saw the rattler slither away. She drew a deep, shuddering breath, and cried out, "Mama! Mama!"

The pain grew worse, and she cried louder for her mother.

Within a few seconds, Corrie rushed up and saw the bucket on the ground and Peggy gripping the calf of her left leg.

"Peggy, what's wrong?" she said, kneeling beside her.

"A rattlesnake bit me!"

Corrie took one look at the bleeding bite, stood up, and looked toward the field where her husband was working. She could see him in the distance, and cupping her hands about her mouth, she shouted his name.

Gilbert heard her and dropped the shovel in his hand as he ran toward the sound of her voice.

Corrie knelt down and examined the bite again. "Peggy, your papa's coming. We've got to get you to the wagon where I can lance the bite and suck out the poison."

Peggy's eyes bulged and she tried to speak, but fear locked her throat.

"Don't try to talk, honey. My lancing the bite won't hurt any worse than it hurts right now. The poison has got to come out."

They heard Gilbert's pounding feet as he drew up. His eyes were bulging as he saw Corrie holding on to Peggy's bloody leg.

"What happened?" he gasped.

"A rattlesnake bit her!" Corrie said. "If you'll carry her to the wagon, I'll run ahead and get ready to lance the bite and suck out the poison."

Moments later, with Peggy lying on the tailgate of the covered wagon, her mother lanced the bite and began to suck the mixture of blood and poison from the wound, repeatedly spitting on the ground. All the while, Gilbert held Peggy's hand and did his best to comfort her.

"Gilbert, climb up into the wagon and get me a strip of cloth out of the top drawer of the cabinet," Corrie said. "I've got to bandage the bite. There's no way to know how much poison may have spread through her bloodstream. We've got to get her to the clinic in Tahlequah as fast as possible."

Gilbert quickly returned with the cloth. While Corrie bandaged the bite, he placed the harness on the team of horses and hitched them to the wagon.

A few minutes later, Corrie was holding a semiconscious Peggy in her arms on the wagon seat while Gilbert had the team galloping toward Tahlequah. All the while, Corrie was praying aloud, asking God to spare her daughter's life. Gilbert kept his eyes on the road, pushing the horses as fast as they could go.

When they reached the Tahlequah Clinic, Dr. Wendell Dixon and Dr. Cary Hines went to work on Peggy. The anxious parents were seated in the waiting room, and Gilbert wrung his hands while Corrie held on to one of his arms and prayed aloud, asking God not to let Peggy die.

After the doctors had been working on Peggy for over half an hour, they left a nurse with her and went to the waiting room. Dr. Dixon, the older of the two, said, "Mrs. Gerson, your effort to suck out as much poison as possible was certainly good, but Dr. Hines and I fear that too much poison may have made it into her system and...well, she may not make it."

Corrie gasped and struggled to get her breath.

"Dr. Hines, would you get her a sedative please?" Dr. Dixon said.

As Dr. Hines headed down the hall, Gilbert said, "Dr. Dixon, I'll go to my daughter's side while you're caring for my wife."

Gilbert entered the small room where Peggy lay on a bed with a nurse at her side and found that his daughter was conscious. Terror was in her eyes. Gilbert took hold of her hand. "Honey, don't be afraid. You're going to be all right."

Peggy rolled her head on the pillow. "No, Papa! I'm not going to be all right!"

"Mr. Gerson," the nurse said in a strained voice, "when Dr. Dixon and Dr. Hines stepped from the room into the hall, Peggy heard them say that she hardly had any chance of surviving."

Gilbert's chest seemed to cave in. He bent over the daughter he loved with all of his heart, and tears welled up in his eyes.

Peggy looked up at him and said weakly, "Papa, you...you told Mama not to talk to me about Jesus. I'm about to die, Papa, but I'm not ready to die. Shall I follow your atheism, or should I follow Mama's faith in Jesus?"

Gilbert Gerson's voice quavered as he said, "Peggy, my atheism has no hope for you. You should follow your mother's faith in Jesus. I'll go get her right now."

When Gilbert reached the waiting room where Dr. Dixon was just finishing giving Corrie the sedative, he stood over her and said, "Honey, Peggy is dying and she knows it. She asked me if she should follow my atheism or if she should follow your faith in Jesus. I told her she should follow your faith in Jesus."

Corrie quickly rose to her feet. She had noticed a Bible lying on a nearby table, and without a word, she picked up the Bible and dashed from the room.

Some thirty minutes later, Corrie returned to the waiting room where Gilbert was sitting alone, his face ashen.

Gilbert stood up, breathing hard. "Is she—is she—?"

"Still alive?" Corrie asked quietly.

"Yes."

She nodded. "Our little girl is still alive. Both doctors are with her again."

Gilbert wiped a shaky palm over his face.

Corrie looked him in the eye and said, "Peggy just put her faith in Jesus Christ as her Saviour, Gilbert, and now, when she dies, she will go to heaven."

Gilbert wiped tears from his eyes and said, "Thank God."

Corrie's brow furrowed. "What did you say? Thank *who*?"

Sniffling, Gilbert wiped away more tears. "I said thank

God. Oh, Corrie, I've been such a fool! I know God exists and that His Son is Jesus Christ. Please…please show me in that Bible what I have to do to be saved."

twenty-one

The Tahlequah Clinic's two doctors had left Nurse Evelyn O'Brien to watch over Peggy Gerson while they tended to other patients. Evelyn was standing over Peggy, giving her a drink of water from a cup, when Gilbert and Corrie Gerson entered the room. Peggy spotted them as she took her last sip and managed a weak smile.

"It's my parents," she told the nurse.

"How's she doing, ma'am?" Gilbert asked as they moved up to the bed.

"Well, from what Dr. Dixon and Dr. Hines told me when I came on duty, she's still quite weak. I've been giving her water to keep her from dehydrating. She just drank a full cup."

Corrie took hold of Peggy's hand. "I love you, honey."

Peggy managed another weak smile. "I love you, too, Mama."

"I have another patient to look in on a few doors down the hall," the nurse said. "My name is Evelyn O'Brien, and I'll be back shortly, but if you should need me before I return, just tell the nurse at the desk, and she'll get word to me."

"We'll do that, ma'am," Gilbert said. "Thank you."

After the nurse left the room, Gilbert bent down and kissed Peggy's forehead. "I have something to tell you."

Peggy fixed her gaze on her father's face. "You look different, Papa. Your eyes…"

"I *am* different, honey. I'm no longer the fool that you've known all your life."

Peggy glanced at her mother and saw tears in her eyes and a smile on her face. "What do you mean, Papa?" she asked, looking back at her father.

Tears welled up in Gilbert's eyes. "I've known all these years that God existed, but I was so wicked and foolish that I didn't want to admit it. When your mother came back to the waiting room and told me that you had received Jesus into your heart, I was so glad to hear it. I told her that I know God exists, and I asked her to show me in the Bible what I had to do to be saved. She did, and I received Jesus into my heart as my Saviour."

Peggy's face wreathed itself in delight. "Oh, Papa, I'm so glad! When I die, I'm going to heaven, and I'm so glad to know that both you and Mama will be there with me someday."

Tears ran down Gilbert's cheeks as he took hold of Peggy's and Corrie's free hands. "I'm not going to be very good at this, but I want to pray and ask God to make you well."

Gilbert's prayer was short and to the point as he asked God to spare Peggy's life, saying he knew He had the power to do so.

When he closed the prayer in Jesus' name, Corrie wrapped her arms around him, and said, "I know God heard you, and I have this peace in my heart that He's going to heal Peggy and spare her life."

Just then Dr. Cary Hines stepped into the room. "I heard you praying, so I waited outside till you were finished. I want to check on Peggy again."

The doctor listened to Peggy's heart with his stethoscope, took her temperature, and checked her pulse. Then he said to the parents, "There is definite improvement here. I can't make you any promises yet, but she's definitely doing better."

Evelyn O'Brien came in at that time, and Dr. Hines shared the good news with her. The Gersons were then asked to return to the waiting room so Peggy could get some rest. Gilbert and Corrie kissed Peggy's cheek and left the room.

When the Gersons sat down in the waiting room, they held hands and talked optimistically about Peggy's situation, then prayed together once more.

Twice during the afternoon, Evelyn came into the waiting room and told the Gersons that the doctors had just checked Peggy and that she was showing improvement and resting well. Gilbert and Corrie praised the Lord together.

At sundown, the Gersons looked up to see both Dr. Dixon and Dr. Hines enter the room with smiles on their faces.

"Mr. and Mrs. Gerson, we stand amazed," Dr. Dixon said.

"We just did a thorough examination of your daughter again, and she has fully recovered. There's only one word to describe it. It's a miracle! God answered your prayers. We can tell by Peggy's heartbeat, the lucidity of her mind, and the clearness of her eyes that the rattlesnake's poison is gone. She's going to be fine."

Moments later, the Gersons left the clinic with Gilbert carrying Peggy. When they reached the wagon, Corrie climbed onto the driver's seat, and Gilbert placed Peggy on the seat next to her. Corrie put an arm around Peggy and said, "I'd like for us to go by the Claiborne home and tell Cherokee Rose that both you and Peggy have been saved today."

Gilbert smiled up at her. "Of course."

"That's good, Mama," Peggy said. "Mrs. Claiborne will be happy to know that by leading you to the Lord, she also had a part in Papa and me becoming Christians."

When the Gersons arrived at the Claiborne home, Peggy walked between her parents as they stepped onto the porch. Gilbert knocked, and seconds later, the tall silver-haired police chief opened the door.

"Chief Claiborne, I'm Gilbert Gerson and this is my wife, Corrie, and our daughter, Peggy. We've come by to give your wife some good news."

"Well, come on in," Britt said, smiling. "My wife is just finishing up the dishes, but she'll be glad to see you."

The Gersons were seated in the parlor, and Britt hurried to the kitchen to tell Cherokee Rose who had come to see her. Seconds later, they entered the parlor together. Corrie stood up and hugged Cherokee Rose, then introduced Gilbert and Peggy.

"We have something to share with you," Corrie said.

They all sat down together, then Corrie told the Claibornes the story of Peggy's being bitten by the rattlesnake, of them taking her to the Tahlequah Clinic, and how the Lord used the incident to bring both her husband and her daughter to Himself.

Cherokee Rose's eyes filled with tears, and there was joy in the Claiborne parlor.

"If you folks can stay here a little longer," Britt said, "I'll go to Pastor Joshudo's house and tell him what has happened. I know he'll want to come and talk with you."

"Sure, we can stay," Gilbert said.

"I can whip up some sandwiches for your supper, if you would like," Cherokee Rose said.

Gilbert and Corrie exchanged glances, then Gilbert said, "Mrs. Claiborne, we'd be delighted. Thank you!"

Britt left to go to the parsonage, and Cherokee Rose took the Gersons into the kitchen.

Some forty-five minutes later, the Gersons were sitting in the parlor with Pastor Joshudo and his wife, Alanda, as well as the Claibornes. The pastor and Alanda listened eagerly as the Gersons told their story.

When they finished, Pastor Joshudo said, "Doesn't our God do marvelous things? Just think about it, Cherokee Rose…the Lord used your father's death to give you the opportunity to lead Corrie to Jesus, then He used the snakebite to make it so both Peggy and her father would hear the gospel and be saved!"

Heads were nodding and all were smiling. The pastor's words about her father's death brought tears to Cherokee

Rose's eyes, but the smile never left her lips.

"The stars are bright tonight!" Britt said.

Gilbert cocked his head and looked at the police chief. "Why do you say the stars are bright tonight?"

Britt then told the story of the Cherokee Chief Sequoyah using those words to express the joy in his heart that the Cherokee people were happy in their new home in Indian Territory. He explained that those were Chief Sequoyah's last written words the night he died in August of 1843.

"My husband uses Chief Sequoyah's words quite often when he is happy about something," Cherokee Rose said. "And we have a Christian settler friend named Craig Parker who has started using them, too. You will get to meet Craig and his wife, Gloria, who are members of our church."

Before the Gersons headed for home, Pastor Joshudo led the group in prayer, praising the Lord for drawing Gilbert, Corrie, and Peggy to Himself, and for sparing Peggy's life.

On the next Sunday, May 12, the Gersons came forward after the sermon to be baptized, and Pastor Joshudo told their story to the congregation. After the baptism, people lined up to welcome the Gersons into the church. When Craig and Gloria Parker and Britt and Cherokee Rose Claiborne drew up to the Gersons, Britt introduced the two families to each other.

Gilbert smiled, shook Craig's hand, and said, "The stars were bright last night, and they will be bright tonight, too!"

Craig laughed and said, "You must have heard the police chief say that."

"Chief Claiborne used those words Friday night, and he told us about Chief Sequoyah."

"I figured it had to be something like that," said Gloria, her eyes shining.

Cherokee Rose stepped up to them and said, "Britt and I want to invite the Gersons and the Parkers to our house for Sunday dinner."

Corrie's eyebrows arched. "That's awfully nice of you, but maybe we should wait till another time. That's five extra mouths for you to feed."

"I always prepare far more food for Sunday dinner than Britt and I can eat. That's because almost every Sunday we invite someone over. I love to cook, and I love having guests in our house."

"It doesn't do any good to argue with her, Mrs. Gerson," Gloria Parker said. "Craig and I have learned that. You might as well take her up on the invitation."

Twenty minutes later, the five guests stepped up on the front porch of the Claiborne cabin, and the delicious aroma from the kitchen greeted them. The cabin's windows were open on that glorious spring day, and a slight breeze fluttered the snowy white curtains.

The men made themselves comfortable in the parlor, while the women and Peggy made their way down the hall toward the kitchen. Corrie paused just inside the kitchen door to look the room over, and for just a moment, the homey kitchen made her homesick for her Kansas home. She sighed deeply.

"Anything wrong, Corrie?" Cherokee Rose asked.

"It's just that being in such a charming kitchen makes me long for the day when I can live in a house again and have a

kitchen of my own. I'm getting tired of preparing meals outside over a fire. Oh, I'm grateful to be here and have our
farmland, but I'll be a lot happier when I can have a kitchen
and a solid roof over my head.

Cherokee Rose smiled. "I remember well when we first
arrived here from North Carolina. My mother died on the
journey, and my father and I had to sleep in a tent. And I had
to do the cooking outside over a fire, too. That's why this cabin
means so much to me. You *will* have a house built soon, won't
you?"

"Gilbert is going to build it as soon as he can. And it can't
be any too soon for me!"

Cherokee Rose hugged her and then held her at arm's
length. "Well, while you're here, I want you to enjoy my
kitchen. Now, we'd better get busy and help Gloria and Peggy
get the food dished up, or we're going to have some hungry
men invading this kitchen!"

Soon dinner was on the table, and after Britt led in prayer,
they all dug in. There was much happy talk during the meal.
By the time dinner was over, Gilbert Gerson shed tears as he
told the group he never realized how wonderful it was to be a
child of God and a part of the "Jesus crowd."

The next day, some five miles due south of Tahlequah, two
neighbors—Jess Holcomb and Harold Talbert—were arguing
at the spot where their property lines joined beside a dusty
road.

"Don't you lie to me, Talbert!" Holcomb said, his eyes
ablaze. "You stole one of my Hereford calves and butchered it!

I found the head and the hide over there in a ditch on your property!"

Talbert clenched his fists at his sides and narrowed his eyes. "I did no such thing, Holcomb! It's not my fault that whoever stole your calf left the head and hide in one of my ditches!"

The two men saw a teenage Cherokee boy hurrying along the road on foot, and he had a troubled look on his face as he watched the two men argue.

Talbert turned from Holcomb long enough to call out, "Hello, Benardo. Don't worry about us. Just a little misunderstanding, that's all."

The boy nodded and kept on going.

"You're gonna pay me for that calf you stole, Talbert, or else!" Holcomb said.

"I told you it wasn't me who did it, and I ain't paying you one thin dime!"

Holcomb whipped out a long-bladed hunting knife from under his belt and buried the blade in Talbert's chest. Talbert collapsed to the ground, and Holcomb bent down and felt for any sign of life. There was none.

As Holcomb stood, he saw another neighbor, Russell Seglund, riding his horse along the road. Seglund was just meeting up with the Cherokee boy, who was still in sight as he hurried along the road.

Panic gripped Jess Holcomb. Russell could see him plainly now, and Holcomb knew he would see the body of Harold Talbert lying at his feet.

When Russell Seglund drew up, Holcomb took off his hat and ran shaky fingers through his hair.

Seglund pulled rein and quickly dismounted, his eyes fixed

on Talbert's lifeless body. "Jess, what happened?"

Holcomb made his voice quaver as he said, "I was walking across my field when I heard Harold arguing with a Cherokee boy I've seen around these parts. His name's Benardo, and I saw him plunge this knife into Harold's chest. Then he saw me coming and took off."

Seglund's eyes were fixed on the corpse. "I'm not acquainted with Benardo, but I did see a Cherokee boy not far from here. That must've been him. He must live in Chief Orodi's village just down the road."

"Yeah, I think that's where he lives."

Seglund pulled at an ear. "I think it would be best if we go to Police Chief Britt Claiborne about this. You can tell him what you saw."

"Yeah, I'd be happy to."

twenty-two

olice Chief Britt Claiborne was at his desk at police headquarters in Tahlequah when there was a tap on the door. He looked up from the papers he was working on and said, "Come in, Najuno."

Officer Najuno opened the door and said, "Chief, there are two settlers here who have asked to talk to you."

"All right. Send them in."

Britt rose to his feet and circled the desk as the two men entered the office. "What can I do for you, gentlemen?"

The men introduced themselves as Jess Holcomb and Russell Seglund. Then

Holcomb said, "There's been a murder, Chief Claiborne. A Cherokee Indian killed my neighbor. I knew you'd want to know about it."

The chief gestured toward the two wooden chairs that faced his desk. "Please sit down."

As Holcomb and Seglund seated themselves, Britt rounded his desk and sat down on his chair. "Who was this neighbor of yours that was murdered?"

"Harold Talbert," Holcomb said. "He was a widower and lived alone on his hundred-and-sixty acres, which is adjacent to mine."

Britt nodded. "I see. Tell me what happened."

Jess Holcomb told Britt that he saw the Cherokee teenager stab Harold Talbert and that the knife he found in Talbert's chest was a Cherokee hunting knife, the kind with a horse bone handle with a Cherokee insignia carved in the bone.

Russell Seglund told the chief he saw the Cherokee boy running away from the stabbing scene as he came riding along the road.

Holcomb then said, "Chief, I'm sure this boy lives in the village led by Chief Orodi, which isn't far from my place. I've seen him around the area, and I once heard someone call him Benardo."

Britt looked at Holcomb silently for a few seconds, then asked, "Is Talbert's body still there in the field with the knife in his chest?"

Holcomb nodded. "I left Harold Talbert just the way I found him."

Britt stood up. "All right. I want to see the body before I do anything else."

—◠—

Britt Claiborne and the two settlers rode up to the spot where Harold Talbert's body lay. They dismounted, and Britt knelt beside the body and examined the knife handle and the blood on Talbert's shirt around the blade. Then he rose to his feet and turned to the two settlers. "I want both of you to tell me your stories of this incident again."

Jess Holcomb frowned. "What for, Chief?"

"I want to get every detail fixed in my mind."

When both men had told their stories the second time, Britt looked at Russell Seglund. "Then you did not see the stabbing. Benardo was already on the road, leaving the scene when you came along on your horse."

Seglund nodded. "That's right."

Britt turned to Holcomb. "And you actually saw Benardo stab Harold Talbert, then run away?"

"Yes, sir. With my own eyes. I heard them arguing just before the Indian whipped out his knife and plunged it into Harold's chest."

Britt stared at him, his eyes gleaming coldly. "Jess Holcomb, you are lying through your teeth. And you're under arrest for the murder of Harold Talbert."

"Wh-what? How can you arrest me? Benardo did it. I *saw* him stab Harold!"

The police chief shook his head. "Benardo could not possibly have done it."

"Why couldn't he have?" Russell Seglund asked.

"I've known Benardo and his parents since he was a small child. When Benardo was a young boy, he fell out of a tree and landed on his neck and shoulders. Benardo can walk, but he cannot so much as move his arms, his hands, or his fingers. He's never carried a knife. He couldn't use one if he had to. There's no way he could've committed this murder."

Britt fixed his eyes on Holcomb. "You're lying to cover your own crime. Why did you stab Harold Talbert? And where did you get that Cherokee knife?"

Jess Holcomb felt an icy chill come over him. He could not find his voice. As the piercing eyes of the police chief locked him in his stance, all he could hear was his own sharp breathing.

Russell Seglund looked on in shock as the police chief spun Holcomb around and handcuffed him, saying, "You're going to jail."

The next day, the *Cherokee Phoenix* carried the story, and less than a week later, under Cherokee law, Jess Holcomb was hanged for his crime.

In late May, rainstorms came almost daily in Oklahoma District as farmers, done with planting their crops, were building their houses and barns.

Before May had passed, funnel clouds were seen twice, and one of the tornadoes struck a freight train as it was crossing the District carrying various supplies to the merchants. Two railroad cars were destroyed, but none of the crew was hurt.

By the end of May, most of the settlers' houses had been built, and their attention was then on finishing their barns and sheds.

—〇—

On Tuesday, June 4, Pastor Joshudo of the Tahlequah church was calling on white settlers who had visited the services. When he arrived at a farm owned by the Erickson family from Kansas, he noted that the farmer, his wife, and their two small sons were behind the house where they were building their barn. Rafe Erickson's wife, Nellie, was struggling to help him lift a heavy beam from a pile of lumber onto a flatbed wagon.

Joshudo overhead Rafe say, "Honey, guess I'll have to get some neighbors to help me with this beam."

It was Billy, their four-year-old, who first noticed the preacher riding toward them and cried out, "Papa! Mama! Pastor Joshudo is here!"

Rafe and Nellie turned around, and both smiled when they saw the pastor riding up.

"Come down off your horse and stay awhile, Pastor," Rafe said.

Joshudo dismounted, and Rafe shook hands with him.

"I have been making some calls this morning, seeing folks who have visited our services lately, and since I was riding right past your place, I wanted to stop and tell you again how happy I am that you joined the church last Sunday."

Rafe smiled. "Well, thank you, Pastor. Nellie and I were so glad when we moved here to find a good Christ-exalting, soul-winning church so close by."

"Yes, we really love the church," Nellie said.

"An' Bobby an' me sure like our Sunday school class, Pastor Joshudo!" Billy said.

The pastor ruffled Billy's hair. "That makes me happy!" He then glanced at the large wooden beam on the lumber pile and said, "You need some help getting that beam on the wagon?"

"It's the beam that goes at the top of the roof, Pastor," Rafe said. "I've got a pulley rigged up there that'll make it easy to bring up, once I've got it on the wagon so I can get it over there. The pulley ropes only come down to the level of the wagon bed."

"Well, I will be glad to help you," Joshudo said.

"All right. I'd sure appreciate it."

Nellie and the boys watched as Rafe and the pastor walked to the beam. Before Rafe even touched it, the preacher took hold of the beam at the center and hoisted it into his arms.

Rafe's eyes popped. "How'd you get so strong?"

Joshudo grinned. "Oh, when I was in my teens, I did a lot of lifting on our farm. My father had injured his back, so it was up to me to do the heavy lifting. Then when I was in my twenties, I joined the Cherokee wrestling team in our area."

"I'd noticed your build before, Pastor, but I didn't realize just how strong you are."

"Well, I might need your help to lift this beam onto the wagon."

Rafe chuckled. "I doubt it, but I'll help you anyway."

When the beam was in place on the wagon, Joshudo told the family that he needed to get back on the road to make his visits. Rafe and Nellie thanked him for his help, and he mounted up and rode away.

A little while later, Joshudo was riding past a farm and saw two young Cherokee men off their horses, talking to the farmer's wife as she stood on the front porch. There was obvious fear on her face.

Joshudo guided his horse onto the property and toward the house just as the woman said in a shaky voice, "I have no food or money to give you. Please leave me alone!"

One of the Cherokees said, "Since you white people have been given our land, you should share your good fortune with us!"

Joshudo quietly pulled up behind the two Indians who stood facing the farmer's wife, then caused them to jump when he said in a loud voice, "You two have no right to talk to this lady in such a manner!"

Both young men gave Joshudo a scornful look, and the huskier one bellowed, "You have no right to stick your nose in our business just because you are a preacher!"

Joshudo dismounted, stepped up to the troublemakers, and said, "Get on your horses and ride!"

"You will not do anything to us!" the huskier one said. "You are one of those Christians, and a preacher, too!"

"Just because I am a Christian and a preacher does not mean I am to stand by and watch the two of you frighten this lady. Now, do as I said. Get on your horses and ride!"

The huskier one took two steps toward Joshudo and swung a fist at him. Joshudo dodged the fist and countered with a blow to his jaw that snapped his head back and lifted him off the ground. He fell in the dust, rolling his head back and forth groggily.

The other one came at Joshudo, fists pumping. Joshudo outmaneuvered him and landed first a left, then a right to his jaw. The young Cherokee went down on his back, out cold.

The farmer's wife drew Joshudo's attention as she bounded off the porch and cried out, "Mike! Mike!"

Joshudo saw a man and two teenage boys running toward the house from the field that bordered the road.

When they drew up, she said, "Those two Cherokees came riding in here while I was on the front porch and demanded that I give them food and money. I think they were going to harm me!"

"We were coming to the house for lunch when we saw what this other Indian did," said her husband, pointing at Joshudo.

The farmer extended his hand and smiled. Joshudo met his grip, and as they were shaking hands, the farmer said, "Sir, my name is Mike Rogers. I want to thank you for protecting my wife."

"Honey, this dear man is a preacher!" the farmer's wife said.

Mike Rogers set curious eyes on Joshudo. "You're really a preacher?"

Joshudo glanced at the huskier Cherokee, who was now kneeling over his friend, trying to wake him up, then met Mike's gaze and said, "I am Pastor Joshudo. You have seen the church in Tahlequah with the steeple that has a cross at its top?"

"Oh, yes," Mike said. "The Cherokee church."

"I am pastor of the church, Mr. Rogers, but many white people also come."

The huskier Cherokee helped his now-conscious friend to his feet. They gave Joshudo a petulant look, then made their way on wobbly legs to their horses. Without a word, they mounted up and rode away.

Mike Rogers turned to his wife. "I don't think they will be coming back here any time soon."

She smiled. "Seems to me that Pastor Joshudo taught them a lesson they won't forget."

Mike turned to the preacher and introduced his wife, Carole, and their sons, Leonard and Douglas.

"I want to sincerely thank you for coming to my rescue," Carole said.

"It was my pleasure, Mrs. Rogers," Joshudo said.

"It's lunchtime, Pastor," Carole said. "Can you stay and eat with us? I have beef sandwiches already made up, along with some fried potatoes. I had just stepped out on the porch to see if Mike and the boys were coming in for lunch when those two men rode into the yard."

"Well, thank you, Mrs. Rogers. I am a bit on the hungry side."

"Good! You men and boys come on inside and get washed up. I'll have some nice cool tea on the table when you're ready to sit down."

Moments later, when the Rogers family and their guest sat down at the large kitchen table, Carole said, "Nothing fancy, Pastor Joshudo, but it will fill all of our stomachs."

"It looks great to me, ma'am." Joshudo ran his gaze over the faces of the family. "Do you mind if I lead us in prayer and thank the Lord for the food?"

"Go ahead, Pastor," Mike said.

They all bowed their heads and as soon as the amen was said, the food was started around the table.

As they were eating, Pastor Joshudo said, "This moment reminds me of a verse in the Bible."

Mike's eyebrows arched. "Really?"

"Yes, Matthew 25:35. 'For I was an hungered, and ye gave me meat: I was thirsty, and ye gave me drink: I was a stranger, and ye took me in.'"

Mike chuckled. "Well, that *does* fit, doesn't it? You're very welcome, Pastor. It's our pleasure to have you in our home."

"Mr. Rogers, it would be my pleasure to have you and your family come and visit our church."

Carole's eyes lit up. "Can we do that, Mike?"

"Of course."

"We haven't been to church since we left Iowa," Douglas said.

Joshudo looked across the table at Mike. "So you have gone to church in the past?"

Mike cleared his throat. "Uh…not regularly, like we should have."

Joshudo was praying in his heart for wisdom. "Mr. Rogers, let me ask you this. If you were to die at this very moment, would you go to heaven?"

Mike's features flushed. "Well…uh…I couldn't say for sure, Pastor. The church where we used to go from time to time did preach about knowing Christ as Saviour, but we didn't come to that place in our lives."

"But we would like to," Carole said.

"I have a Bible in my saddlebags," Joshudo said. "As soon as we finish lunch, would you let me show you how to make Jesus your Saviour so you can *know* you're going to heaven when you leave this world?"

"Certainly," Mike said. "We each have a Bible, but they're still packed in a box in the boys' room. We can get them out."

"Good! Then you can all follow along in your Bibles while I read to you from mine."

When the meal was over, Mike Rogers went to find their Bibles while Pastor Joshudo hurried outside to get his out of his saddlebags. Carole and the boys cleared the dishes from the table, and the Rogers family and Pastor Joshudo sat around the table, each with a Bible in hand.

Since the Rogers family had heard the gospel before, it took Pastor Joshudo only about thirty minutes to lead all four of them to the Lord.

twenty-three

n Sunday morning, three families who had come to faith in Christ just that week came forward at the end of the service to be baptized: the Mike Rogers family, Bruce and Shelley Watson and their teenage children, Bruce Jr. and Nancy, and Ralph and Maryann Byers and their teenage daughter, Lydia.

Before the three families went to the dressing rooms to prepare to be baptized, Mike Rogers asked the pastor if he could say something to the people. Mike told them what the pastor had done on Tuesday to the two men who were being rude to his wife, and said, "Folks, I can really understand how it is that Pastor Joshudo scares people into coming to church."

There was hearty laughter all over the auditorium.

After the baptismal service, members of the church welcomed the new families. As the families mingled and talked, fourteen-year-old Nancy Watson and thirteen-year-old Lydia Byers began to get acquainted and decided to ask their parents if they could spend some time together. The parents happily approved.

The Watsons and the Byerses decided to go to Tahlequah together later that week to do some shopping, and on Friday morning, June 14, Ralph and Maryann Byers took Lydia with them to the Watson place. They left Lydia and Nancy Watson there to have some time together, and the parents and Bruce Jr. headed for Tahlequah in the Watson wagon.

The girls had been talking for some time in the parlor, sitting on the sofa by the large parlor window, when dark, heavy clouds rolled in and the sky came alive with lightning bolts that cracked one after the other. A strong wind began to blow, thunder shook the house, and rain began to fall in sheets.

Lydia began to tremble and to rub her upper arms as she stared out the window.

Attempting to cover her own fright, Nancy put an arm around her new friend and said, "Don't worry, Lydia. We'll be fine."

Lydia noted the slight tremor in Nancy's voice. "Should we go some place safer in the house?"

Nancy stood up. "Maybe we should get farther from the window but stay here in the parlor so we can keep an eye on the storm."

Lydia rose to her feet, and the girls stepped backward a few paces, their eyes still glued to the spectacle outside. They sat down side by side on straight-backed wooden chairs near the parlor door.

Nearly an hour later, the wind became stronger and the clouds much darker. Suddenly Nancy and Lydia were startled to see a funnel take shape and drop down out of the sky from one of the dark clouds, moving toward them from the west.

Nancy jumped to her feet, her eyes bulging. "Lydia, that's a tornado! And it's headed straight this way!"

Both girls dashed out of the house in search of a low spot outside. They were running toward a ditch as the swirling, roaring tornado drew closer.

It was raining hard in Tahlequah. The Watsons and the Byerses were inside the town's new hardware store and gathered at the large window with other customers and the store's personnel to watch the black funnel cloud to the west.

Shelley and Maryann clung to their husbands, fearful for Lydia and Nancy and their properties.

Bruce Watson looked at the others and said in a tight voice, "Let's pray right now."

The five of them held hands in a small circle while the others in the store looked on, and Bruce prayed aloud, asking the Lord to protect Lydia and Nancy and their homes.

In less than half an hour, the tornado had turned south and gone out of sight. The rain was also letting up. The two families climbed into the Watson wagon, and Bruce put the team to a gallop.

On the streets of Tahlequah, people gathered in small groups, talking fearfully about what damage might have been done by the tornado west of town.

The clouds were beginning to break up as the wagon moved up the last gentle rise before the Watson place would come into view. When they topped the rise, they all saw that the Watson house, barn, and toolshed had been destroyed.

"The girls! I don't see the girls!" Maryann wailed.

"Oh, dear Lord, please!" Shelley said. "Nancy! Lydia!"

A moment later, Bruce pulled the team to a skidding halt. Ralph Byers and Bruce Watson jumped to the ground and went to the rear of the wagon to help their wives down over the tailgate.

"Our team and wagon are nowhere in sight," Ralph said.

"Maybe the horses took off when they saw the storm coming," Maryann said.

"We've got to find Nancy and Lydia!" Bruce said.

All five of them searched through the piles of broken lumber and sections of roofing and walls where the house once stood, but found nothing.

"Let's spread out," Ralph said.

Bruce, Shelley, and Bruce Jr. headed for the shambles that had once been the barn, and Ralph and Maryann hurried to where the toolshed had stood.

Suddenly Ralph's attention was drawn to a deep ditch a few yards away, and he went closer to investigate. "Look, Maryann, it's Nancy!"

Ralph shouted over his shoulder to the Watsons, "Hey! Nancy's here in this ditch!"

Ralph stepped down into the ditch and bent over Nancy. At first he thought she was dead, but his eye caught the rise and fall of her chest. "She's alive!" he cried out. Quickly, he gathered her into his arms, and as he was climbing out of the ditch, the Watsons drew up beside Maryann.

"She's unconscious," said Ralph as he carried the girl toward her parents and brother. "There's a bruise on the left side of her face where something must've struck her. Probably knocked her into the ditch."

Bruce extended his arms toward Ralph. "I'll take her."

Ralph placed the girl in her father's arms, and Shelley moved close, her brow furrowed as she focused on her daughter. Bruce Jr. was at her side.

Nancy began to move her head and moan. She opened her eyes and focused on her father's face. "Papa! Oh, Papa!"

Shelley burst into happy tears and kissed her daughter's cheek. "Thank You, Lord! Thank You!"

"Nancy, do you know where Lydia is?" Shelley said.

Nancy looked at her mother. "No, Mama. I…I don't know what happened to her."

Bruce looked at Shelley. "Honey, I'll lay her down on the ground here. You stay with her while Junior and I help Ralph and Maryann look for Lydia."

Shelley nodded and knelt beside her daughter. She looked up at the Byerses with misty eyes. "I'll be praying for Lydia."

Maryann bit her lower lip. "Thank you."

Bruce and his sixteen-year-old son went one direction and the Byerses went another.

Ralph and Maryann followed the ditch, and some twenty yards from the spot where Nancy had been found, they saw a splintered wall from the toolshed lying over the top of the ditch. As they drew close to it, suddenly they heard a faint cry from underneath.

"Ralph!" Maryann shouted. "That's Lydia's voice!"

Bruce Watson and his son heard Maryann's shout and came on the run.

Ralph was in the ditch, attempting to lift the wall when Bruce arrived and jumped down beside him. Together they raised it up and placed it on one side of the ditch.

Lydia was struggling to get up. Ralph gathered her into his arms, and she broke into sobs, crying, "Papa! Papa!"

Within seconds, Ralph had Lydia out of the ditch, and both parents embraced their daughter, weeping for joy and praising the Lord.

A quick examination revealed that Lydia had not been harmed. She told them that she and Nancy had been running alongside the ditch, searching for the best place to hide, when pieces of wood and tree limbs came flying through the air. She had been running ahead of Nancy, and when she looked behind her, Nancy was not there. She immediately jumped into the ditch, though it was not very deep at that spot. Just as she hit bottom and lay down, the section of roof landed above her.

Her face pinched as she asked, "Is Nancy all right?"

"She is, honey," Maryann said. "She got a bruise on the side of her face. Some flying object apparently hit her and knocked her unconscious. We found her in the ditch back there a ways, but she's awake now. She's fine."

"Oh, I'm so glad, Mama. I want to go see her."

The girls were brought together and hugged each other, and the parents and Bruce Jr. praised the Lord that neither one was seriously hurt.

Shelley then turned and looked at the destruction of the barn, then the house. She began to weep. "Oh, Bruce, it's all gone! We've lost everything!"

Bruce wrapped her in his arms. "Honey...we can build again. It's not the end of the world."

Shelley looked up at her husband, tears streaming down her cheeks, and tried to swallow her sobs. "But we've worked so hard since we came here. We got the house, barn, and tool-shed built, and now they're gone. It's almost more than I can take."

Bruce squeezed her tight. "It'll be all right, sweetheart. With God, all things are possible. He will help us."

Shelley let those words sink in, then eased back in her husband's arms and managed a slight smile. "You're right, darling. The God who saved our souls can certainly see us through this problem. The main thing is that our precious Nancy is all right. The Lord certainly took care of her in the storm."

"Yes, He did. And He will take care of our family the rest of the way, too."

Ralph and Maryann were softly whispering to each other. Then they stepped up to Bruce and Shelley. "We know you still have your covered wagon," Ralph said, "but we want you to come home with us. You can stay in our house until you get your new one built."

Bruce and Shelley looked at each other, then back at their friends. "I guess we'll take you up on that," Bruce said. "Thank you so much."

Bruce looked at the Byerses. "I sure hope your horses headed for home when they saw the storm coming."

Ralph sighed. "Yeah, me, too."

Both families loaded into the Watson wagon, and they moved westward along the muddy road. The sun shone down from a sky now dotted with small white clouds. Ralph and Maryann spoke words of comfort to Bruce and Shelley in an attempt to help them in their loss.

When they drove past the Parker farm, Ralph said, "Looks like the tornado missed Craig and Gloria's place."

"I'm glad for that," Bruce said. "Looks like most of the farms around here are intact."

Soon, all that stood between the wagon and a clear view of the Byers place was a large stand of trees. Just as they passed the trees, Maryann gasped and put her hand over her mouth. "Ralph! Our buildings are gone, too!"

The three teenagers inside the wagon scrambled up to the canvas opening and looked past their parents at the destruction where the Byers house and barn had stood.

The Watsons stared silently at the scene as Maryann took hold of her husband's arm. "Oh, Ralph, what are we going to do?"

Ralph cleared his throat with his own eyes fixed on the jumbled piles of lumber and pieces of furniture scattered over the area. "Honey, we'll…we'll do the same thing our friends here are going to do. With the Lord's help, we'll rebuild."

"But we put everything we had into the house and barn. We won't have any money until it's time to harvest our crops. And I don't see any sign of our horses and wagon."

Ralph took hold of her hand as Bruce was drawing the wagon to a halt near the spot where the house had stood.

"Honey, I don't pretend to understand all of this, but the Lord had a reason for letting it happen. The Watsons and us need to pray together and seek His guidance. But let's remember that we have much to be thankful for. The Lord spared our girls when they might easily have been killed."

When everyone was out of the wagon, Bruce said, "Ralph is right. We need to pray together and ask the Lord to guide us in all of this." He turned to Ralph. "Lead us, will you?"

The small group joined hands, and Ralph Byers led them in prayer, thanking God for sparing Nancy and Lydia and asking Him for His guidance, His help, and His mercy in this time of difficulty in their lives.

When Ralph closed his prayer, he said to the others, "Since the Parkers are our Christian friends, I think we should go tell them what happened. I believe they would want to know."

The Watsons and the Byerses arrived at the Parker place and told them of their misfortune. Craig and Gloria were deeply sympathetic and very glad that both girls were all right.

Craig and Gloria spoke to each other in whispers. Then Craig turned and said, "Gloria and I will make room for both families in our house until you can get your new houses and outbuildings built."

Bruce shook his head. "Oh, we can't ask you to do that."

"You're not asking," Craig said with a smile. "We're telling you that we want you to stay here just as long as you need to. It may be a little crowded, but God has admonished His children to care for one another. We'll make do. Don't you worry. Our Lord will provide."

"That's right," Gloria said. "You are our brothers and sisters in the Lord, and we love you."

Ralph's brow furrowed. "We love you, too, but this may take a long time. Maryann and I don't have enough money to rebuild. We'll have to wait till the Lord somehow provides it for us."

"We're in the same situation," Bruce said. "Craig... Gloria...we just might wear out our welcome."

"No way," said Craig, shaking his head. "Gloria and I would give both families the money you need if we had it, but maybe Pastor Joshudo will lead the church to help you."

"Oh, we can't ask the pastor to do that, Craig," Ralph said.

"Well then, I will go to Pastor Joshudo and tell him what has happened and see what he says."

"But—"

"No, no," Craig said. "Christians are supposed to take care of each other. I'll ride my horse to town right now and talk to the pastor about this."

The next Sunday morning, Pastor Joshudo stood at the pulpit and told his people about the destruction at both the Watson place and the Byers place. He explained that both families were now living with the Parkers. He then asked those who could help in a financial way if they would do so. A few people, Indian and white, raised their hands, saying they would do what they could.

After the service, Lee and Kathy Belden hurried to the two

families and handed Bruce and Ralph each a generous check, drawn on their account at the Tahlequah Bank. Moments later, Britt and Cherokee Rose told the two families they would take what they could from their small savings account and give it to them. They told them they would bring it to them at the Parker place on Monday afternoon. Others approached with offers of help, including Gene Vader, Martha Ackerman, and the Will Bakers.

Just as the Watsons, the Byerses, and the Parkers were about to head for home, Pastor Joshudo and Alanda came up to them and announced that they were going to give them a portion of his salary each week until they no longer needed it.

Tears flowed as they were thanked.

As the Parkers and their houseguests headed for the Parker wagon, Shelley Watson said in a voice filled with amazement, "What wonderful Christian friends we have! I'm going to pray that the Lord will bless them abundantly!"

Maryann smiled. "Maybe someday the Lord will allow us to be a blessing to someone else in need. That's what Christian love is all about."

"Indeed it is," Ralph said.

"Bless them one and all!" Bruce said with a lump in his throat.

Time moved on. In June of 1890, Pastor Joshudo performed the wedding ceremony for Gene Vader and Martha Ackerman at the church. The Bakers were pleased to see their widowed daughter and her children fully happy again and living in the comfortable house Gene had built.

By the end of July 1890, the Byerses and the Watsons finally completed their new houses and outbuildings and moved back to their properties. The small amount of money from Pastor Joshudo and Alanda continued to come to them weekly, but they still struggled financially. Craig and Gloria wanted to help them, but were having a hard time with their own finances.

All three farms, however, were producing enough crops to make each family a meager living, and because the Byerses' horses and wagon had never been found, they had to squeeze enough money from their income to purchase a new team and wagon.

twenty-four

n the fall of 1890, with things running relatively smooth in Oklahoma District, Chief U.S. Marshal Robert Landon and the deputy marshals returned to their respective places. Law-keeping, then, was solely in the hands of the Cherokee Nation police force and the United States army at Fort Gibson.

By the summer of 1893, the Beldens were doing quite well on their 160 acres. The creek that ran through their property supplied ample water for their crops. Daily, during Bible-reading and prayer time in their home,

Lee and Kathy and their sons thanked the Lord for Craig and Gloria Parker and their unselfishness in letting them have that prime piece of land. The Beldens often had the Parkers over for supper, and the two couples became close friends.

The Parkers were not as fortunate with their land, and at times were pinched financially. Some of their livestock had died from a virus that swept through the herd. In spite of this, they still had a burning desire to help their neighbors, the Byerses and the Watsons, who had had to borrow money from the Tahlequah Bank to rebuild their houses and outbuildings. Though the people of the church were no longer giving them money, Pastor Joshudo had the church praying for them and for the Parkers.

One warm summer day, Craig Parker walked across his land examining his crops. He was strolling through a grassy section spangled with orange, purple, and bright yellow flowers. He was talking to the Lord about his and Gloria's tight finances when he noticed a dark wet substance trickling through a tiny groove at the bottom of a dry gully. He stepped down into the gully, bent over, and stuck his fingers in the thick liquid. Standing up straight, he rubbed his fingers together and raised the wetness to his nose and smelled it. A thrill of excitement caused him to shake all over.

"It has to be oil!" he exclaimed aloud. "It's *got* to be oil! What else could it be?"

He climbed out of the gully and ran to the house and into the kitchen. He reached into one of the cupboards and took out an empty canning jar, then hurried out the back door and ran back to the gully. He went to the bottom again, let the trickling black substance run into the jar until it was nearly full, screwed the metal lid on, and ran back to the house.

When Craig entered the kitchen this time, Gloria was there. She looked at the canning jar in his hand and asked, "What do you have there?"

Craig stepped up to her with a broad smile on his face and unscrewed the lid. "Stick a finger in it and tell me what you think it is."

Gloria stuck her forefinger into the black substance, raised her hand close to her face, and rubbed her thumb and forefinger together. She looked at her husband. "Where did you get this?"

"In a gully out by the cornfield. It's running in a tiny stream at the bottom of the gully."

Gloria brought it up to her nose and sniffed it. "I...I think it's oil," she said, meeting Craig's gaze.

"That's what I think, too."

"It sure feels like oil and smells like oil."

"I'm going to take this jar to Britt. If he thinks it's oil, I'm going to ask him what to do next."

Gloria was moving up and down on her toes. "Go! Quick!"

A half hour later, Craig rode into Tahlequah, drew up in front of police headquarters, and dismounted. He took the jar from the saddlebag and hurried inside.

"Hello, Mr. Parker," Officer Najuno said. "What can I do for you?"

"I need to see Chief Claiborne."

Najuno rubbed his chin. "Well, sir, Chief Claiborne is sort of tied up right now. He is in his office with Cherokee Nation authorities. I...I do not think he would mind if I told you what is going on, since you two are such good friends."

Craig's eyebrows raised. "What?"

"Well, sir, the authorities are telling him that because of his age, he must retire from the police force. They say he is getting too old to carry on as police chief."

Craig nodded slowly. "Do you think they'll be at it much longer?"

"Probably not. They have been in there for almost an hour. I expect they will be through soon."

"All right. I'll wait."

Craig sat down in the outer office, and it was almost half an hour before the Cherokee government leaders came out. Najuno ushered Craig to Britt's office, and Craig quickly showed Britt the black liquid in the jar, telling him where he had found it. Britt looked at the liquid, smelled it, and squeezed a few drops between his fingers.

"What do you think it is?" he asked, smiling at Craig.

"Gloria and I both think it's oil."

"I would say so, too, but the best thing for you to do is take it to my son-in-law, Landry Lovegren. He's now president of the Williams Park Oil Company, and it won't take him long to find out if this is oil. And if it is…"

"If it is, Gloria and I will be out of our financial troubles."

"Let me know as soon as you get back, won't you?"

"I sure will!"

Early the next morning, Craig rode his horse toward Wichita Falls, Texas. As he rode, he thought of the many things he could do, not only for Gloria and himself, but for their friends as well. At one point, he drew rein in a grove of trees, dismounted, and took a long drink of water from his canteen. Then reaching into the saddlebag, he took out the jar of black liquid and dropped to his knees, bowing his head.

"Lord, if this is oil, I promise You that not only will we tithe to our church, but we'll also share this bounty with others. You know my heart, and You know Gloria's. We're Your servants. We will help those dear friends of ours who are under financial stress. I love You, Lord Jesus. Amen."

Craig sensed a calming peace steal over him. He placed the jar back in the saddlebag, mounted up, and put his horse to a gallop.

Late in the afternoon, Landry Lovegren's secretary ushered Craig into his office. Landry stepped around his desk and shook hands with Craig. "Hey, my friend, it's good to see you again! What brings you to Wichita Falls?"

Craig handed Landry the jar and told him he had found the black substance on his property and needed to know if it was oil. Landry took Craig to one of the company's technicians, and when a simple test was done, it was confirmed that it was indeed oil.

Landry made arrangements with Craig to begin drilling on the Parker land. Williams Park Oil Company would then purchase any oil they found from the Parkers at a fair price and have it shipped in barrels to Wichita Falls by railroad. Papers were drawn up and signed, making it official.

When Craig arrived home, he told Gloria that it was indeed oil and explained his arrangements with the oil company. Then Craig told her he had thought of a problem while riding home.

"What is that?" she asked.

"Well, honey, we haven't been on this land for five years…just a little more than four. By law, we won't be given title to it until we've been here for five years. Right now, the oil beneath this land belongs to the District."

"I think you should go talk to Britt Claiborne about it," Gloria said.

"I was just thinking the same thing."

In little more than half an hour, Craig was with Britt in his office and told him what he had learned and explained the arrangements he and Landry had made. Craig then told Britt that he and Gloria did not yet have title to the property. By District law, they had almost a year to go.

"I think there's a good chance that you and Gloria could be granted legal possession sooner than the required five years," Britt said. "Let's go talk to the U.S. government official here in Tahlequah who has jurisdiction over Oklahoma District. I'll tell him how you unselfishly sacrificed that other parcel of land to the Beldens, and let's see what he says."

When the government official heard the story about the Parkers sacrificing the land with the creek running through it to the Beldens, and Britt also told him about Craig and Gloria's desire to help the Byerses and the Watsons recover from the devastating tornado, the official granted the Parkers title to the land immediately.

Within five weeks, oil derricks were scattered all over the Parker place, and soon pumps were bringing oil out of the ground in great amounts.

As Craig and Gloria drove their wagon toward home on the day they had deposited their first oil company check at the Tahlequah Bank, Craig turned to Gloria and said, "Well, sweetheart, I think we should go by the Watson place and the Byers place and invite them for supper this evening. It's time we tell them what we're going to do."

Gloria took hold of his arm and squeezed it. "I can hardly wait!"

That night, the Parkers stood in front of their house and watched the Watsons and the Byerses drive away in their wagons beneath a silver moon.

Gloria looked up at her husband with a smile. "What a blessing it was to make those dear people so happy!"

"And it will continue to be a blessing with every check we give them," Craig said.

"I can hardly wait till tomorrow evening when we have the Claibornes over and tell them our plans for their future."

The next evening, Britt and Cherokee Rose talked with Craig and Gloria over supper about how well things had gone for them.

"May I remind you," Britt said, "that I told you when you gave up that choice piece of land to the Beldens that your unselfishness would be blessed by the Lord? Well, He has done it, hasn't He?"

"Yes, He has," Craig said. "And do you and Cherokee Rose remember what I said at that time?"

They both looked at Craig blankly.

"Britt, when you said you believed that the Lord was going to bless us in a big way, I said that if He did, Gloria and I would see if we could share that blessing with you and your dear wife."

"That's right, you did. I remember now," Britt said.

Craig cleared his throat gently. "Britt, I haven't told you, but the day I came to your office to find out if you thought my discovery was oil, you were in a meeting with the Cherokee Nation authorities. I know what the meeting was about."

"Oh?"

"They were talking to you about retiring."

Britt's head bobbed. "How did you know?"

"Officer Najuno told me. He said he felt he could since you and I are such good friends. So when are you retiring?"

Britt grinned. "In two weeks."

Cherokee Rose's face beamed. "Isn't it wonderful!"

"That is wonderful. Congratulations, you two," Gloria said.

"I only recently told Gloria about what Officer Najuno told me that day," Craig said. "We know you're not exactly rolling in money, so we'd like to have the two of you live here on our property so we can help you with whatever you need as you grow older. We want to give you five acres to live on, build you a nice house, and dig you a well. We'll also share our wealth with you so you'll never have to worry about finances."

Britt and Cherokee Rose had tears in their eyes as Britt said, "We've been praying about whether to go live close to our relatives in Texas or stay in Oklahoma District. I'll receive a small pension for my service as police chief, but it won't be enough to live on.

"Up till now, we haven't had peace about moving to Texas. The distance is relatively short between this part of Oklahoma District and where our children, grandchildren, and great-grandchildren live, so we could still see them often. Now I know why the Lord hadn't given us peace about moving there."

Cherokee Rose wiped away the tears now streaming down her cheeks and said in a soft voice, "You know we were married here, oh, so many years ago. Our children were born and raised here, and this land has been our home for so many years. We have enjoyed good times and suffered through bad times. My father's body is buried here. Really, this is where I want to spend the rest of my days with the husband that God blessed me with so long ago."

She looked at Britt, and a slow smile lit up his face. "Then, sweetheart," he said, "this will remain our place to call home until the Lord calls us to our eternal home. Oklahoma District truly is our earthly land of promise!"

Britt looked at the Parkers. "I guess you can see that we're taking you up on your offer."

Both couples shed tears of joy.

After supper, the four of them walked out under the stars, and with joy in his heart, Britt Claiborne put an arm around Cherokee Rose, looked up to the heavens, and said, "Praise the Lord! The stars are bright tonight!"

epilogue

n 1890, tribal leaders of the Five Civilized Tribes attempted to persuade President Benjamin Harrison and the United States Congress to allow the Indian reservations in Oklahoma District to become one of the United States. They wanted to call it the State of Sequoyah, with the capital at Fort Gibson.

This request was quickly denied, and the president and Congress immediately decreed the end of independent tribal law and courts. They set a deadline of January 6, 1906, for the termination of all tribal government.

By the mid-1890s, Oklahoma District had become a major oil-producing region. It became the forty-sixth state of the Union on November 16, 1907, and was then named the State of Oklahoma. At the same time, Oklahoma City became its capital.

As might be expected, the early legal settlers of Oklahoma District held a very low opinion of the sooners. That began to change by 1908, when the University of Oklahoma adopted the name Sooners for its athletic teams. By the 1920s, the term no longer carried a negative connotation, and Oklahomans adopted the nickname as a badge of pride. Although never officially designated as such by statute or resolution, Oklahoma has since been known as the Sooner State.

Travel along the Trail of Tears
A Place to Call Home series

By Al & JoAnna Lacy

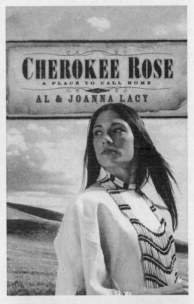

Cherokee Rose—BOOK ONE
ISBN: 1-59052-562-0

It's late summer 1838. President Martin Van Buren issues an order that the fifteen thousand Cherokee Indians living in the Smoky Mountains of North Carolina are to be evicted from their homeland. Forced to migrate to Indian Territory, the Cherokees begin their tragic, one-thousand-mile journey westward. Most of the seven thousand soldiers escorting them along the way are brutally cruel. But Cherokee Rose, an eighteen-year-old Indian girl, finds one soldier, Lieutenant Britt Claiborne, willing to stand up for them. Both Christians, Cherokee Rose discovers that Britt is also a quarter Cherokee himself. It's upon the Trail of Tears that they fall in love, dreaming of one day marrying and finding a place to call home together.

Bright Are the Stars—BOOK TWO
ISBN: 1-59052-563-9

The North Carolina Cherokees are settling into their new home in Indian Territory and Britt Claiborne and Cherokee Rose are settling into married life. Britt, a quarter Cherokee Indian, is released from the United States army and joins the Cherokee Police Force where his position takes him into fearsome and heart-gripping dangers. They raise two children with much love and delight. They also lean on God through the trials of their day—including the death of the popular Cherokee Chief Sequoyah, who had translated the Bible into their language. Follow the historical events that punctuate their lives until 1889, when President Harrison announces that whites are free to enter Indian Territory, now known by the Indians as home.

Frontier Doctor Trilogy

ONE MORE SUNRISE–BOOK ONE

Young frontier doctor Dane Logan is gaining renown as a surgeon. Beyond his wildest hopes, he meets his long-lost love—only to risk losing her to the Tag Moran gang.

ISBN 1-59052-308-3

BELOVED PHYSICIAN–BOOK TWO

While Dr. Dane gains renown by rescuing people from gunfights, Indian attacks, and a mine collapse, Nurse Tharyn mourns the capture of her dear friend Melinda by renegade Utes.

ISBN 1-59052-313-X

THE HEART REMEMBERS–BOOK THREE

In this final book in the Frontier Doctor trilogy, Dane survives an accident, but not without losing his memory. Who is he? Does he have a family somewhere?

ISBN 1-59052-351-2

Hannah of Fort Bridger Series

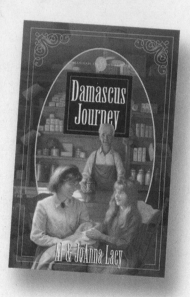

Hannah Cooper's husband dies on the dusty Oregon Trail, leaving her in charge of five children and a general store in Fort Bridger. Dependence on God fortifies her against grueling challenges and bitter tragedies.

#1	*Under the Distant Sky*	ISBN 1-57673-033-6
#2	*Consider the Lilies*	ISBN 1-57673-049-2
#3	*No Place for Fear*	ISBN 1-57673-083-2
#4	*Pillow of Stone*	ISBN 1-57673-234-7
#5	*The Perfect Gift*	ISBN 1-57673-407-2
#6	*Touch of Compassion*	ISBN 1-57673-422-6
#7	*Beyond the Valley*	ISBN 1-57673-618-0
#8	*Damascus Journey*	ISBN 1-57673-630-X

Angel of Mercy Series

Post-Civil War nurse Breanna Baylor uses her professional skill to bring healing to the body, and her faith in the Redeemer to bring comfort to thirsty souls, valiantly serving God on the dangerous frontier.

#1   *A Promise for Breanna*   ISBN 0-88070-797-6
#2   *Faithful Heart*   ISBN 0-88070-835-2
#3   *Captive Set Free*   ISBN 0-88070-872-7
#4   *A Dream Fulfilled*   ISBN 0-88070-940-5
#5   *Suffer the Little Children*   ISBN 1-57673-039-5
#6   *Whither Thou Goest*   ISBN 1-57673-078-6
#7   *Final Justice*   ISBN 1-57673-260-6
#8   *Not by Might*   ISBN 1-57673-242-8
#9   *Things Not Seen*   ISBN 1-57673-413-7
#10 *Far Above Rubies*   ISBN 1-57673-499-4

Shadow of Liberty Series

Let Freedom Ring
#1 in the Shadow of Liberty Series

It is January 1886 in Russia. Vladimir Petrovna, a Christian husband and father of three, faces bankruptcy, persecution for his beliefs, and despair. The solutions lie across a perilous sea.

ISBN 1-57673-756-X

The Secret Place
#2 in the Shadow of Liberty Series

Popular authors Al and JoAnna Lacy offer a compelling question: As two young people cope with love's longings on opposite shores, can they find the serenity of God's covering in *the secret place?*

ISBN 1-57673-800-0

A Prince Among Them
#3 in the Shadow of Liberty Series

A bitter enemy of Queen Victoria kidnaps her favorite great-grandson. Emigrants Jeremy and Cecelia Barlow book passage on the same ship to America, facing a complex dilemma that only all-knowing God can set right.

ISBN 1-57673-880-9

Undying Love
#4 in the Shadow of Liberty Series

Nineteen-year-old Stephan Varda flees his own guilt and his father's rage in Hungary, finding *undying love* from his heavenly Father—and a beautiful girl—across the ocean in America.

ISBN 1-57673-930-9

The Orphan Train Trilogy

THE LITTLE SPARROWS, Book #1

Kearney, Cheyenne, Rawlins. Reno, Sacramento, San Francisco. At each train station, a few lucky orphans from the crowded streets of New York City receive the fulfillment of their dreams: a home and family. This orphan train is the vision of Charles Loring Brace, founder of the Children's Aid Society, who cannot bear to see innocent children abandoned in the overpopulated cities of the mid-nineteenth century. Yet it is not just the orphans whose lives need mending—follow the train along and watch God's hand restore love and laughter to the right family at the right time!

ISBN 1-59052-063-7

ALL MY TOMOROWS, Book #2

When sixty-two orphans and abandoned children leave New York City on a train headed out West, they have no idea what to expect. Will they get separated from their friends and siblings? Will their new families love them? Will a family even pick them at all? Future events are wilder than any of them could imagine—ranging from kidnappings and whippings to stowing away on wagon trains, from starting orphanages of their own to serving as missionaries to the Apache. No matter what, their paths are being watched by Someone who cares about and carefully plans all their tomorrows.

ISBN 1-59052-130-7

WHISPERS IN THE WIND, Book #3

Young Dane Weston's dream is to become a doctor. But it will take more than just determination to realize his goal, once his family is murdered and he ends up in a colony of street waifs begging for food. Then he ends up being mistaken for a murderer himself and sentenced to life in prison. Now what will become of his friendship with the pretty orphan girl Tharyn, who wanted to enter the medical profession herself? Does she feel he is anything more than a big brother to her? And will she ever write him again?

ISBN 1-59052-169-2

Mail Order Bride Series

Desperate men who settled the West resorted to unconventional measures in their quest for companionship—advertising for and marrying women they'd never even met! Read about a unique and adventurous period in the history of romance.

Journey of the Stranger Series

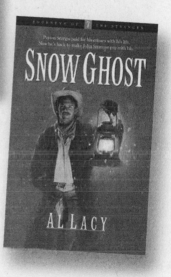

One dark, mysterious man rides for truth and justice. On his hip is a Colt .45…and in his pack is a large, black Bible. He is the legend known only as the stranger.

#1	*Legacy*	ISBN 0-88070-619-8
#2	*Silent Abduction*	ISBN 0-88070-877-8
#3	*Blizzard*	ISBN 0-88070-702-X
#4	*Tears of the Sun*	ISBN 0-88070-838-7
#5	*Circle of Fire*	ISBN 0-88070-893-X
#6	*Quiet Thunder*	ISBN 0-88070-975-8
#7	*Snow Ghost*	ISBN 1-57673-047-6

Battles of Destiny Series

The Battle Begins...

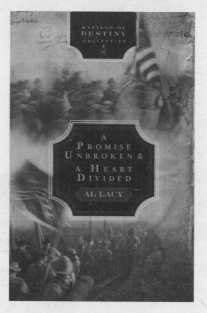

ISBN: 1-59052-945-6

A Promise Unbroken (Battle of Rich Mountain)
As the first winds of Civil War sweep across the Virginia countryside, the wealthy Ruffin family is torn by forces that threaten their way of life and, ultimately, their promises to one another. Mandrake and Orchid, slaves on the Ruffin plantation, must also fight for the desire of their hearts. Heartache and victory. Jealousy and racial hatred. From a prosperous Virginia plantation to a grim jail cell outside of Lynchburg, follow the dramatic story of love indestructible.

A Heart Divided (Battle of Mobile Bay)
Wounded early in the Civil War, Captain Ryan McGraw is nursed back to health by army nurse Dixie Quade. In her tender care, love's seed is sown. But with the sudden appearance of Victoria, the wife who once abandoned Ryan, and the five-year-old son he never knew he had, come threats endangering the lives of everyone involved. Between the deadly forces of war and two loves, McGraw is caught with *a heart divided*.

The Battle Continues...

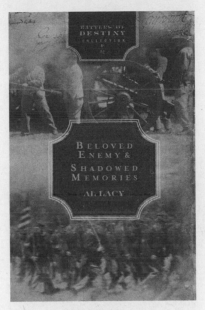

ISBN: 1-59052-946-4

Beloved Enemy (Battle of First Bull Run)
Faithful to her family and the land of her birth, young Jenny Jordan covers
for her father's Confederate spy missions. But as she grows closer to Union
solider Buck Brownell, she's torn between devotion to the South and her
feelings for the man she is forbidden to love.

Overwhelmed by pressure to assist the South, Jenny carries critical
information over enemy lines and is caught in Buck Brownell's territory.
Will he follow orders to execute the beautiful spy... or find a way to save his
beloved enemy?

Shadowed Memories (Battle of Shiloh)
Critically wounded on the field of battle, one man struggles to regain his
strength and the memories that have slipped away from him. Although he
cannot reclaim his ties to the past, he's soon caught up in the present and
the depth of his love for Hannah Rose.

Haunted by amnesia, the handsome officer realizes he may already be
married. And so, risking all that he knows and loves, he turns away to
confront his *shadowed memories*, including those of "Julie"—the mysterious
woman he thinks he left behind.

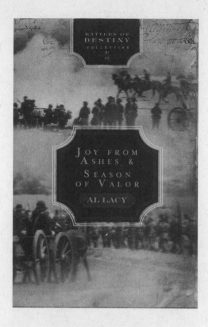

ISBN: 1-59052-947-2

Joy From Ashes (Battle of Fredericksburg)
While fighting to defend his home and family against Union attack, Major Layne Dalton learns that enemy soldiers have brutalized his wife. Tragically, the actions of three cruel-hearted Heglund brothers have caused not only the suffering of his bride, but also the death of Layne and Melody's unborn son. Thirsting for vengeance, the young major vows to bring judgment upon those responsible, yet surprising circumstances make Dalton— presumed dead by his wife and fellow soldiers—a prisoner of the very men he swore he would destroy.

Season of Valor (Battle of Gettysburg)
As teenagers, Shane Donovan and Ashley Kilrain promise to love each other forever. But when Ashley's parents decide to return to Ireland and take their daughter with them, the sweethearts sadly bid each other farewell and accept their fate.

After several years, both have found other loves and married. So when Ashley returns to Maine and the friendship between the two is rekindled, Shane and Ashley find that a new kind of love is needed to overcome the sprouting seeds of tragedy in their freshly intertwined lives.

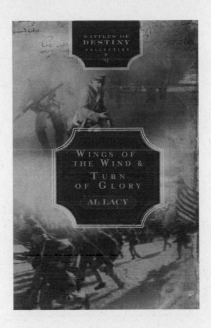

ISBN: 1-59052-948-0

Wings of the Wind (Battle of Antietam)
Early in his life, tragedy and hardship caused young Hunter McGuire to lose everyone he loved: his parents, his little sister, his best friend. Years later, Dr. Hunter McGuire grieves once again after being separated from the young nursing student who has stolen his heart. This time, however, a tender reunion takes place after Jodie returns unexpectedly and helps Hunter tend the wounded at the battle of Antietam. Yet their struggles have just begun, for their life together is threatened by more than they realize. And only One can save their love: the God who walks on the *wings of the wind*.

Turn of Glory (Battle of Chancellorsville)
Confederate Major Rance Dayton is wounded on the battlefield and fears he will die until four friends risk their lives to save him. The courageous four are honored and live as heroes until, in the confusion and darkness of a nighttime battle, an unthinkable tragic accident changes their lives forever. The four, so recently renowned as heroes, are now despised and hounded as miscreants, and soon they desert the army and head west to live as outlaws. It is there that Rance, a newly commissioned U.S. Marshal, meets the four again, this time in very different circumstances, but with the knowledge that he owes them his life.